No Forty-Hour Week

No Forty-Hour Week

Goldie Down

Southern Publishing Association, Nashville, Tennessee

Copyright © 1978 by
Southern Publishing Association

This book was
Edited by Don Short
Designed by Mark O'Connor
Cover painting by Bill Myers

Type set: 11/12 Melior

Printed in U.S.A.

Library of Congress Cataloging in Publication Data

Down, Goldie M.
    No forty hour week.

    1. Ranchi Hospital.   2. Missions, Medical—India—
Ranchi (City)   I. Title.
RA990.I42R473   362.1'1'095412   77-19223
ISBN 0-8127-0167-4

266
40 ✗

Contents

No Forty-Hour Week

Chapter 1

Doing Rounds With Doctor

"Would you like to come with me while I visit my patients?" Dr. Evelyn invited us.

Our family had recently arrived in India, and our minds whirled with a medley of curious impressions: ash-clothed holy men clanging cymbals, spicy curries, chattering monkeys, bazaars full of gleaming brassware, fragrant flowers, creaking bullock carts meandering along dusty roads, minor-key music, colorful crowds of people, and over it all the scorching, enervating heat.

I murmured that I didn't want to be in the way, but she brushed my objections aside and gently urged me toward the hospital door.

Because the sun glaring off the squat, white buildings so dazzled me, I scarcely saw the men squatting on the veranda in the shade of the crimson bougainvillea, chewing betel nut, spitting, and mumbling in low, melancholy voices.

Their silent wives and big-eyed children sat on wooden benches around the walls of the waiting room watching our approach with unblinking stares. They were used to seeing Dr. Evelyn and her husband, Dr. Neale, and Helene, the hospital matron; but their expressions clearly said to David and me, "Who are you? Why are you here?"

I wished that I could explain that David was a pastor who wanted to tell them about Jesus, and the children and I just wanted to love them when and where we could.

11

But I couldn't speak their language, and Dr. Evelyn had already ushered us into the first ward. Four high iron beds took up most of the floor space. Patients' relatives, their pots, pans, odd-shaped bags, bundles of bedding, and foodstuffs occupied the rest. Little clay stoves, chunks of charcoal, and cherished sticks of firewood were stored under some of the beds. Anything less like the orderly, antiseptic atmosphere of the hospital wards with which I was familiar would be hard to imagine.

"It's because of the caste system," Dr. Evelyn hastened to explain. "Each patient has to be accompanied by a relative or someone who will cook his food and care for his personal needs. Sometimes a high-caste patient will not even allow a nurse of a lower caste to give him an injection, and one of us has to give it.

"Of course all this junk shouldn't be in the ward. There is a fine brick kitchen nearby where the relatives are supposed to do the cooking, but there are always some who can't be coaxed or threatened into using it. They insist on kindling the smoky fires and preparing the patient's food as close as possible to his bedside."

I made some noncommital sounds to convey my appreciation of the problems involved, and Dr. Evelyn chuckled. "It takes time to educate people to our ways. One of my predecessors told me that she had once found a live chicken tethered to a bedpost ready to be slaughtered for the next day's curry."

We halted beside the first bed, and Dr. Evelyn took the small patient's hand and helped him to his feet. The little fellow wore nothing but an apprehensive expression, and his big brown eyes and greatly distended stomach made him look like an old-fashioned Kewpie doll.

When I asked what was wrong with him, Dr. Eve-

12

lyn said it was his spleen, then added a lot of technical jargon that I didn't understand. She patted him on the head, and he obediently sat down and pulled the white sheet over his thin sticks of legs.

We stopped only briefly at the next two beds. The fourth bed seemed to be unoccupied, but when we walked closer, I saw a tiny scrap of a baby wrapped in a piece of faded red cloth lying like a stain in the middle of the big white bed. Dr. Evelyn said he had tetanus.

Knowing that tetanus is caused by an open wound coming in contact with fouled soil, I asked how a baby so small could possibly have tenanus.

Dr. Evelyn sighed. "He's ten days old. We have so many tiny babies brought in suffering with tetanus. They are born in the village, and the old midwife cuts the umbilical cord with the same knife that is used to dig potatoes or trim toenails.

"Sometimes it's the mother who gets it. A woman was brought in last week with a three-week-old baby. We gave her massive doses of antitoxin and tried everything we knew, but we couldn't save her."

"What happened to the baby?" I asked.

Dr. Evelyn assured me that the nurses had taught his seven-year-old sister how to care for him and prepare his formula. They gave her the only plastic feeding bottle that the hospital possessed, because they were afraid a glass one might be broken and the infant would starve before his father could go to the nearest big town and buy another one.

We stepped into another ward. "These patients are all burn cases," Dr. Evelyn explained, "and the ward is always full. Because the Indian village women use open fires for cooking, their long saris trail over the flame; or little children play too close and fall into the fire; or the rice boils over and they are scalded. The trouble is that they usually heal up at

13

home with no medical attention, and then months (sometimes years) later they come to us to repair the damage. Look at this poor baby."

A curly-haired tot with her right hand swathed in bandages lay on the bed, and an ayah squatting beside it hastily scrambled up and salaamed as we approached. Speaking quietly, so as not to disturb the sleeping child, Dr. Evelyn told us that the baby's hand had been scalded when she was very young, and her parents had simply wrapped a rag around it and left it. The skin sloughed off, and as young babies habitually keep their fingers doubled up, the hand had healed into a solid mass. When the child was brought in, she had only a rounded lump of flesh at the end of her wrist. The doctor carefully cut the mass back into a semblance of fingers and kept them separated while they healed.

"She's young and her bones are pliable, so there's every hope that she will be able to use her hand in normal fashion," she finished and led us to the door of an adjoining private room.

"The woman in here has cholera. Normally we don't take infectious diseases, but she was so ill when her relatives brought her in that we knew she would not live to reach the infectious-diseases hospital in town. Cholera patients usually die of dehydration because of the constant vomiting and diarrhea, but we gave her large amounts of intravenous fluids, and she's doing fine now."

When Dr. Evelyn patted the thin, brown shoulder, the woman caught her hand and kissed it. Everywhere we went I could see that the patients adored their doctor, and no wonder. Already I was beginning to fall under the spell of this frail, fair woman with the indomitable will to heal.

"I have to see one more patient, a little girl in the family wards." As Dr. Evelyn led the way across the compound, I wondered aloud what a "family ward" was. She explained that it was a self-contained apartment consisting of two bedrooms and a tiny courtyard, with a primitive kitchen and an even more primitive bathroom opening off it. The whole suite cost about fifteen dollars a day, and only wealthy people could afford such luxury.

Upon entering the first room I discovered why the name "family ward." Doting parents, grandparents, uncles, aunts, and cousins surrounded the patient's bed. A covey of servants hovered in the background. In an aside Dr. Evelyn explained that they had all come to stay for the duration of the child's hospitalization and left me trying to work out how they could all sleep in those two tiny bedrooms.

Immediately one of the group saw Dr. Evelyn and alerted the rest, and the hubbub of chatter ceased. The women pressed their soft, bejeweled hands together in polite namaste, and the men bowed and demonstrated their emancipation from convention by coming forward to shake hands.

Dr. Evelyn checked the patient and talked with the relatives for a long time. As we made our way back to the main building she told me about the child. Three years ago, when the little girl was about nine years old, she had been severely burned about the knees and hips. With no medical attention, she had discovered for herself that the pain was easier to bear when she squatted on the floor and kept the air away from her burns. Even when lying in bed she kept her legs pulled up until finally they had healed in a semi-squatting position that left her unable to stand upright. Now Dr. Evelyn was going to make incisions in the groin and back of her knees and do skin grafts in an effort to straighten her legs.

"Come to the operating room tomorrow and watch, Goldie. You'll find it very interesting."

15

I wasn't so sure about that, but I asked quickly, "Why did her parents leave it so long before bringing her for treatment? They look wealthy enough."

"Perhaps they lived in a district where there was no medical care. There are millions of doctors in India, but most of them prefer to live and work in large towns and cities. It could have been apathy. The reason they have brought the child to me now is because she is nearing marriageable age, and her relatives are starting to think of a prospective bridegroom for her. Her father told me that he would pay a handsome dowry, and that would ensure a good match in any case. But he was worried for fear that her crippled condition would prevent her from bearing children to her future husband."

"Mmm," I said. I was learning many things—fast.

Before leaving, we had a Cook's tour of all the hospital buildings and outbuildings and made suitable comments when shown the new operating-theater complex and the newly acquired operating table.

We oohed and aahed over the boxlike dark room for X-ray developing, the tiny laboratory with its microscopes and test tubes, and the shelves and shelves of medicine bottles and pillboxes on the side of the room that doubled as dispensary.

To our uninitiated eyes, the facilities looked rather rudimentary, but we knew very little about what a hospital should look like. We had yet to learn that much of the satisfaction these devoted doctors and nurses, indigenous and foreign, received from their tasks was derived from the tremendous challenge of inventing and making do.

Chapter 2

In the Operating Theater

At seven the next morning my timid knock brought Nurse Nelia to the outer door of the operating theater. The doctors had already been hard at work for more than an hour, and the sickening smell of ether penetrated to the dressing room, making my head swim as I struggled into an unaccustomed gown and cap. When Nelia insisted that I tie a mask over my mouth and nose, I wondered whether I really ought to enter the theater at all. What if I fainted and disgraced myself?

"Can't I watch through the window?" I nodded toward the huge pane of plate glass that formed a wall between the main theater and the two smaller ones used for minor cases.

"You wouldn't see much from there, and Dr. Evelyn said to bring you inside."

Reluctantly I followed Nelia in, and Dr. Evelyn looked up from her task long enough to greet me and tell me to stand on a stool so that I could look over her shoulder and see what she was doing.

"I've nearly finished this appendectomy, and there are a couple of minor operations before we do the skin graft."

I nodded, and soon I was so fascinated by the skill of her rubber-gloved hands and the nice precision of her movements that I forgot to be upset. As there was none of the spurting blood and tangled intestines that I had expected to see, I was able to keep my stomach in its correct position.

When the appendix patient was wheeled out, I stepped off my stool and looked around. The only time I had previously been in an operating room, I was the patient, but this room appeared to be similar to the one I remembered. A huge overhead lamp dominated the ceiling, and mobile tables holding trays of curious-looking instruments and glass jars of cotton balls stood around the wall. An oxygen cylinder occupied the far corner, along with a baby cot and various machines that I could not identify. In the center stood the fine new operating table that Nurse Helene had described as doing "everything but perform the operation by itself."

As my eyes wandered around, they lighted on one alien object, and at the same time I became aware of soft music struggling to be heard above the belligerent hiss of the sterilizing Primus and the muffled din of outside noises. I knew that Dr. Evelyn was wedded to her tape recorder and played it on every possible occasion, but I had not expected her to carry her passion to such lengths. She saw me looking at it and hastened to explain.

"Doctor . . . (I did not catch his name because her voice was muffled by her mask) told me that musical therapy is used a lot in the States. It calms the patients and relaxes the staff; so I decided to try it this morning. But in my hurry I must have picked up the wrong tape."

Tapping her foot in time to the music, she turned to the patient who had just been wheeled in and commented to me, "This woman asked to be sterilized because the family is very poor, and she already has eight children." She made a small incision and continued her commentary: "See, here is the Fallopian tube; I loop it and tie it like this—quite simple."

Watching and listening, I realized why Evelyn

had apologized for bringing the wrong tape. The operation was proceeding to the stately strains of the wedding march.

While the orderlies wheeled the woman back to her ward, the nurses bustled about, removing trays and bloodstained coverings and replacing used instruments with sterile ones. In the middle of all the activity, blood-curdling screams heralded the approach of the next patient—a woman who was to have her tonsils removed.

She yelled as if she were about to be beheaded, and the nurses half carried, half dragged her into the room and helped her onto the table. Helene tried to calm her with kind words and sympathetic pats on her shoulder, but the screams continued unabated. Suddenly the theater door burst open, and in charged a fierce, wild-eyed individual with a huge curved knife in his belt. He strode up to the operating table, scattering nurses right and left. For a few terrified moments I pictured us all being massacred by an ignorant tribesman who thought his wife was being murdered.

Instead, the wild one shouted above her screams and told her to be quiet, emphasizing his order with clenched fists and angry scowls. Like magic the woman's shrieks subsided; but to make sure she made no further fuss, the husband stood by glowering at her and shouting threats if she so much as whimpered.

All sighed in relief when the woman was sent back to the ward along with her fiery husband. The theater was prepared for the skin graft on the little girl.

The child was already sedated and fast asleep when they wheeled her in, and Brother Joshua, who on operation days became chief anesthetist, took up his position at her head. Dr. Neale offered prayer, and the operation began.

First Dr. Evelyn made straight incisions across the groin, severing the tightly drawn skin so that the legs

19

could be straightened out. The thickness of the scar tissue that had grown over the burned area amazed me. It looked thick and tough like cowhide, but Evelyn's tiny scalpel trimmed here and there and made triangular wounds several inches across to release the puckered thighs.

Then Nelia folded back the sheet that covered the child's lower legs, and Dr. Neale picked up a razor blade and began paring off thin shavings of skin and dropping them into a bowl of saline solution.

I broke out in goose pimples. This ghastly flaying procedure was too much for me, and I hastily turned my attention back to Evelyn who was dipping her forceps into the saline solution and picking out tiny scraps of skin and placing them neatly on the exposed flesh.

"Will the patches of skin all grow into one piece and cover her legs?" The patches nowhere touched each other, and I could hardly believe it possible. Dr. Evelyn explained that the child's legs would be bandaged and left for eight days before being opened for the first dressing. By that time the area would be well covered.

"But I don't know how to prevent her from moving her legs until the skin heals," Evelyn pondered as she looked at her husband for the answer.

"Plaster," said Dr. Neale.

"Of course, plaster. But until the plaster dries we will have to do something. She's sure to be restless as she comes out of the anesthetic, and we have to ensure rigidity . . ." Evelyn lapsed into a mumble as she mulled over the problem. Suddenly she brightened. "I know. We can put a stick between her knees to keep them apart. Brother Joshua, will you find one?"

With the operation finished and the child swathed in bandages from hip to ankle, I took off my cap and gown and went with Evelyn and the nurses as they

20

carried the little girl back to her bed in the family ward. The plaster bandage was to be put on in the ward so that the theater would be free for Dr. Neale to proceed with his listed surgeries.

Dozens of pairs of curious brown eyes watched our progress. When we reached the room and put the child onto the bed, all the relatives crowded around. As many onlookers as could push their way inside stared wide-eyed as Dr. Evelyn wound plaster-impregnated bandages around the child's legs and splashed water on them so that the plaster would set.

The audience had obviously never seen anything like this before. Nurse Nelia wiped a plastery hand across her forehead, making a zebra pattern on her dark skin, and they chuckled their appreciation.

When Dr. Evelyn fitted a piece of thick doweling stick between the little girl's knees and plastered it into position, the crowd really goggled. Dr. Evelyn explained to the relatives that the success of the operation depended on the girl's legs being kept perfectly still until the plaster bandages set firmly.

The legs healed without incident, and a few weeks later the girl, able to stand upright and walk in a normal manner, left the hospital.

Chapter 3

Babies

Whether deliberately planned or not, Dr. Evelyn's invitation to watch her doing rounds got me involved. The day following the skin graft my thoughts still wandered back to the patients I'd seen at the hospital.

Whenever I looked at our baby son I wondered if the tiny scrap of humanity in the middle of the high white bed still struggled for life. Dr. Evelyn said they'd already given him forty thousand units of antitoxin, and I couldn't figure how they could inject so much into such a tiny baby without the needle going right through him.

I thought about the old woman with cholera, the Kewpie boy with his swollen spleen, the burn cases, but especially the tetanus baby. I simply must find out whether he still lived.

I suggested a walk to the hospital, to the delight of our children. They loved to go and play with the doctors' three children, and trudging a half mile in the searing heat of midafternoon meant nothing to them. While they ran off to the doctors' bungalow, I self-consciously braved the scores of expressionless brown eyes staring at me from wards and verandas and went to the ward where I had seen the tenanus baby.

Peeping around the door, I saw the tiny red bundle in the center of the high bed and the baby's mother crouched motionless beside him. For a few minutes I watched, then tiptoed quietly away. I decided to ask Dr. Evelyn about him, and I found her in the nursing office busily working with charts and records.

"Oh, he's improving." Her eyes shone with the light of victory. "It's a miracle. We've never had a tetanus baby recover before."

I rejoiced with her, and then she told me about another baby that had been saved that morning. Dr. Sen, from town, had brought a sick baby and its parents out to the hospital for consultation. He could not decide what was wrong, and neither could Dr. Evelyn, but the baby—limp and scarcely breathing—seemed as if any gasp could be his last.

Evelyn started artificial respiration while the nurses prepared hot and cold baths. They gave him intravenous glucose, and as they worked the staff prayed. "It was prayer that saved him," Dr. Evelyn ended. "Even Dr. Sen admitted that."

"Is the baby completely better now?"

"Better? He was completely cured of whatever ailed him. We kept him here for a few hours of observation, and then his parents took him home."

Dr. Evelyn tapped her pen on the desk and reflected aloud, "But it doesn't always happen like that. We had three babies die on the same day last week."

"Three?" I couldn't keep the horror out of my voice.

Dr. Evelyn shrugged sadly. "Often the relatives wait too long before they bring their sick to us. One baby died at the door before the parents even entered the waiting room. Another one was blue when his mother rushed him in to me. I tried to save him, even though I could see it was hopeless."

"And the third?"

"I really don't know what was wrong with the third baby. The poor little mite was only skin and bones when I examined her, and her mother seemed vague about symptoms—she could have been suffering from any one of a number of ailments. In spite of

23

our treatments she was gone before the end of the day.

"The mother was very philosophic about it. She was seven months pregnant and already had a baby for every year of her marriage; so I suppose she would hardly miss one."

I wanted to know whether the mother would have grieved more if the baby had been a boy, but Dr. Evelyn assured me that the old prejudices were fast dying out, especially among educated people. Preference for boys is only because of the economic situation. It costs so much for a dowry and wedding that if there is more than one girl in the family, the parents can usually afford to marry off only the older one. The others have to remain unmarried.

While I was digesting that information Evelyn laughed and began another anecdote. "Last week the *bania's* (grocer's) wife came into the hospital for her ninth baby, and just for fun one of the junior nurses asked her if she did not want to have it adopted out, seeing that the family was so poor and she had eight others at home. But bania's wife didn't think it funny. She sat up in bed, fat shoulders heaving indignantly, and declared loudly that every new baby was welcome in their home. Poor things, I don't know how they feed the tribe they have now, and it's against their religion to practice birth control."

I murmured something about the combination of poverty and ignorance being so pitiable, and Dr. Evelyn cut me short by claiming that ignorance was not confined to the poor people. Then she told me about a visit she made to the home of an Indian colleague whose wife had six-month-old twins. He complained that the babies cried almost constantly, and Dr. Evelyn immediately said that they must be hungry. She asked why he didn't order supplementary feeding with dried-milk preparations and easily digested cereals. He just shrugged and said that he knew she

24

was right, but there was nothing he could do. His wife's mother and all the other female relatives would raise the roof if he even suggested such a thing. Custom decreed that the twins be fed nothing but milk until they reached a certain age.

"But couldn't he feed them secretly—in his own home?" I asked.

Dr. Evelyn smiled at my ignorance and explained that although the Indian way of life has much to recommend it, the custom of whole families living in the same house, or as close together as possible, has disadvantages. Often a son marries and brings his wife home, and his mother takes charge of her and their subsequent children. Unmarried brothers and sisters live in the same house, along with incumbent grandparents, uncles, aunts, or other more distant relatives.

"Don't worry," she reassured me. "I think he'll find some way around the problem. It's the grandparents with their old customs who hold the country back. Most of the young generation are educated about germs and hygiene and nutrition, and they know which customs to drop and which to retain.

"Yesterday a man brought his wife back to me for postnatal check. I congratulated them on their bonny son, a beautifully healthy babe, and the man beamed and said, 'Thank yourself, doctor. We have done everything exactly as you advised us, and the baby is your testimonial.'

"And a worthy testimonial he was too." Evelyn smiled with exaggerated smugness, and we both laughed as I left her to her records and went off to collect my children from her bungalow.

Chapter 4

Murder in the Village

"Well, I think that's the last of them settled down now, and I hope no babies decide to arrive tonight—I could do with a rest." Nurse Lela rubbed her forehead with a weary hand and sat down at the large desk to record the treatments and medications given since she came on duty. Behind her a nurse's aide locked the drug cupboard and handed back the keys.

"Thank you. Would you check on the woman in room 21, nurse? She had surgery this morning, and she's very restless."

The girl nodded and disappeared in the direction of the wards. Lela could hear the whisper of her soft-soled shoes on the concrete veranda until distance swallowed up the sound, and heavy silence descended, broken only by an occasional groan or snore from the blackness beyond the nursing office.

Lela laid down her pen and felt in her handbag for the sweater she was knitting. Half an hour ticked slowly by as her busy needles clicked to the tune of the passing seconds on the stern-faced old clock staring down at her from the wall above the window. The premature baby in a cot near her elbow hiccuped, and far away in a distant corner of the hospital compound the night watchman called eerily as he made his rounds.

"Soon be time to feed the baby." She spoke aloud as if the sound of her own voice helped to dispel the loneliness of the nursing office. She put her knitting down on the desk, the scarlet wool making a bright spot in the severely white room as she addressed her next remarks to it. "I don't know why I bother bringing you with me. I never get more than half a dozen rows knitted any night, even when it's quiet like this, and none at all when we're really busy. Oh, well!" She bent over the baby's cot, then straightened in sudden alarm at the sound of running feet.

Three men dashed around the corner and halted abruptly at the door of the nursing office, their hurricane lantern swinging uselessly in the brighter light. "Ring for the police," the leader croaked harshly. "There's been a murder."

A wild-looking fellow clothed only in a G-string and a dirty shawl pushed him aside. "Two murders," he blurted.

Lela's eyes widened in horror, and her heart pounded madly. Two? Why not another—with herself as the third victim? These primitive, half-naked men looked capable of anything.

Striving to appear calm, she lifted the receiver off its hook and ran her finger down the list of emergency numbers handwritten on tattered, yellowed paper and taped onto the telephone: the list had been there as long as she had been at the hospital, and this was the first time she had used it.

"Two-three-seven," she said when the operator answered, and turning back to the men she asked, "Kahar [Where]?"

"In our village." Three shaggy heads nodded in the direction of the hospital's back wall, and the third disheveled individual leaned toward her and hissed, "He said she was a witch and killed her. Tell the police to come quickly." His heavy, odorous breath and blood-red mouth told of betel-nut addiction, and Lela shuddered.

"How did it happen?" She replaced the receiver and sat down. Her fear was draining away; if she

27

could only keep them talking until the police came—

As if she had pressed a button, all three began speaking at once, their voices growing louder and louder as the tale unfolded. Patients' relatives sleeping on the verandas uncurled themselves and came to listen. The nurse's aide returned and joined the group, her mouth dropping open in fear and astonishment. The noise and commotion attracted the night watchman's attention, and he ran up, bamboo *lathi* (nightstick) at the ready. Ambulatory patients left their beds in order to get to the root of the matter, and in a few minutes the hospital was ablaze with lights and humming with speculation. Soon the whole story was pieced together.

"Ram's baby is sick." The women nodded to one another. "*Aribahb* [It is very sick]!"

"Have they rubbed hot ashes on its stomach?" A tall, gaunt woman in a faded green sari folded her angular legs under her and squatted in the dusty village square where the others gossiped. Ordinarily the women would have been out in the fields working alongside their men while their naked brown babies were minded by older, but only slightly bigger, brothers or sisters, who romped and played, seemingly oblivious of the burdens tied to their little backs. But rice planting had just finished, and everyone had time on his hands until the transplanting should begin.

"*Jee* [Yes]," the others answered her. "Hot ashes and many other things Ram's wife has tried, but still the baby screams."

"The gods . . . ?" An old granny sucked toothlessly at her lower lip as she made the suggestion.

"Ram himself made an offering to the gods"—a young girl tossed her head, and her tawdry dangling earrings tinkled delicately— "I saw him at the temple

28

with a chicken and rice and a little saffron powder."

"I know that mustard oil, warmed and rubbed over the heart, works wonders. When Basu's son was ill . . ."

So the women talked on, their shrill voices softened with sympathy as they searched their minds for other remedies that could be tried on the sick baby.

The narrow, crooked village street—banked on either side by straggling rows of mud-brick houses—was only a few hundred yards from the back wall of the mission hospital, but no one suggested taking the sick baby to the hospital. All the villagers knew that the hospital was there. They had all heard of the kindhearted nurses and doctors. They were all aware that no one was turned away, even if he was too poor to pay for treatment. But generation after generation of ancestors had lived—and died—in their village without the benefit of doctors or hospitals. The thought of seeking outside help never entered their minds. They simply sat back and waited to see what would happen.

And happen it did. The baby became worse—and worse. Its cries gave way to feeble moans. In vain Ram's wife pressed the infant to her breast. He made no effort to suck, and his little head drooped limply over her arm. Too weak now to stir, his tiny limbs grew pale and cold, and in a short time the wasted body stiffened in death.

Ram's wife, shrieking in an agony of despair, threw her sari over her head. The waiting, listening women covered their faces and wailed in sympathy. Ram got up and walked heavily out of the hut. He deeply loved his small son, and the child's death was a great blow to him, but it was beneath his masculine dignity to show grief.

As he stalked past the group of weeping, whispering women he caught one word, *witchcraft*. Instantly he stopped. The idea penetrated his brain like a shot arrow.

Witchcraft! That was it. A spell had been cast on his child. What else would cause it to die so suddenly?

"Who?" he demanded of the assembled women. "Who cast the spell?"

There was an uneasy silence. The women ceased their noisy weeping and stared at him. They had not thought that far ahead. No one spoke, until suddenly an old hag, moved with sudden inspiration, nodded toward Ram's hut. "The baby's grandmother," she hissed. "The old crone, she has done nothing all day but sit in the corner and mutter."

Ram stood stock-still, his dull mind working slowly. His own mother? Surely she loved her little grandson too much to do such a thing! But did she? Ram resented the fact that his parents were now too old to work in the fields, and yet they lived on and on. He and his brother Jotin had to feed and clothe them while they, his mother especially, were always interfering in his affairs and telling him to do this or that. Many times he had spoken rudely to her and threatened to deny her food unless she minded her own business. Could she have taken vengeance by casting a spell on his son? The evil eye—no one knew who had it!

Seized by sudden fury, Ram pushed his way through the crowd of inquisitive villagers and reentered his hut. His wife was still sitting with the dead child across her knees, wailing and rocking back and forth in grief. In the darkest corner of the room his mother crouched, swaying and muttering to herself, in senile oblivion.

Ram strode toward her and grabbed her by the arm. "You put a spell on my son," he shouted. The old woman looked vacantly up at him. Her toothless

30

mouth opened and shut, but no sound came. Ram jerked her to her feet and shook her until her hoary head rattled on her skinny neck. "You killed him," Ram shouted again. "I'll kill you." Still she stared at him, helpless and uncomprehending. His anger mounted.

Catching up the dead child, Ram's wife stopped weeping and fled from the hut. She had seen Ram in a black rage before, and there was no knowing what he would do. Outside the door she met her brother-in-law returning from his work in the fields. "Ram is killing your mother," she whimpered as she ran to seek refuge in a neighbor's hut.

Jotin threw down his wooden plow and hurried inside.

"Witch!" Ram was yelling as he shook his mother again. "You witch! I will kill you." Throwing her to the floor, he rushed to the back of the hut to fetch his knife—the sharp heavy knife that he used for digging roots, lopping off branches, or slaughtering animals. It was sticking in the thatched roof just under the eaves, and as he reached for it his aged father appeared behind him.

"What's the matter, Son?" He laid a gentle hand on Ram's shoulder. "Why do you accuse your mother of casting spells? The child's death had to be—it is fate. Perhaps the gods are angry . . .?"

"Get out of my way," Ram roared, turning on him with upraised knife. The old man dodged aside and Ram plunged into the hut, straight to the corner where his old mother lay in a trembling heap. Savagely he struck again and again while Jotin held their father at bay.

When the old woman's screams were silenced, Ram turned to his father, who was struggling to free himself from Jotin's grasp. "Be quiet, or you will be the next to die."

31

"You murderer," his father sobbed. "You un-natural son. You have killed your own mother."

"Quiet!" Jotin ordered. "The old witch deserved all she got. I'm tired of working to feed you good-for-nothing old ones anyway."

"Murderer!" The old man blazed. Wrenching himself from Jotin's grasp, the old man fell on Ram, clawing and tearing with his bare hands. "Murderer!"

Jotin sprang to his brother's rescue and held his father while Ram drove home the knife. The old man's accusations died away in a dreadful gurgle, and his sons flung him into the corner to die alongside his wife. Then, grabbing up some food, the brothers dashed out of the house and ran to hide in the rocky hills behind the village.

Lela slept all the next day, and when she reported to the nursing office at 10 PM, she wanted to know the sequel to the story.

"Did the police come out about those murders?"

"What?" asked the day nurse absently as she signed off duty. "Oh, you mean the old couple who were killed in the village last night? Yes, they sent two constables out about three o'clock this afternoon. But the gatekeeper said he saw the bodies still lying by the side of the road at suppertime."

"But did they catch the sons who murdered them?"

"Oh, no, they had about a fifteen-hour start on the police. I expect they will hide away for a month or two until it all blows over, and then they'll come home again. Life is cheap in the village."

Chapter 5

To Everything a Season

We were at the hospital discussing plans for a proposed outing when the subject came up. Someone suggested a certain date, but Dr. Neale shook his head. "No, I wouldn't feel free to leave the hospital then because it's the fracture season, and I might be needed at any time."

"Then how about August or September?"

Again Dr. Neale shook his head. "That's not really suitable either. There'd still be the likelihood of rain because the monsoon would not be finished by then, and besides, that's about the middle of the baby season, and Evelyn would need to stay by the hospital."

Fracture season? Baby season? I opened my mouth to say something but changed my mind. After all, one doesn't want to display one's ignorance in front of a man, even a gentleman like Dr. Neale. But as soon as I could, I elbowed Helene off into a private corner.

"What's all this about a fracture season and a baby season, Hel? I know typhoid and cholera are seasonal because they're endemic and spread in the summer with all the flies and that, but surely fractured bones are not contagious?"

Helene's eyes twinkled. "The fracture season begins when the first mangoes and litchis ripen. We get a real epidemic of broken bones in the fruit season."

"I hadn't thought of that. But a baby season? I thought babies arrived all year around."

She smiled. "Of course they do, but we have more

33

maternity cases about ten or eleven months after harvest than at any other time of the year."

Seeing that my face was one big question mark, she explained that most of the village weddings take place when harvesting is finished and the grain is either stored or sold. Then the villagers have time to make all the arrangements and enjoy the tamasha (the visiting and music and feasting which goes on for days).

"After he's sold part of his harvest is the only time a farmer has enough money to spend on getting a son or daughter married off; they're poor most of the rest of the year."

"I hadn't thought of that either." I turned to rejoin the group, but Helene hadn't finished educating me yet.

"We have a definite season for operations too."

"Oh, come on, Helene, you're joking."

"No, I'm not. Urgent operations are performed at any time, of course, but if it is something chronic that can be postponed without danger to the patient, then he always asks for it to be done in winter."

"Why ever is that?"

Helene smiled at my ignorance and asked with pseudoscorn, "Don't you find it more pleasant to snuggle up in bed in winter than in summer?" And when I nodded, she continued, "So do the Indian patients. I think they feel the heat even more keenly than we foreigners, and they can't bear the thought of being swathed in bandages or plaster casts and lying in bed in the sticky summer heat."

"Very wise, indeed."

"The doctors like it better, too, because there is less risk of infection in the winter, not so many flies around, and all the usual epidemics like dysentery and cholera and so on are not so prevalent in the cool weather."

34

"There's a season for everything. Do you have any more seasonal diseases?"

"Not that I can think of right now, but if you want to have special attention, plan to come into the hospital around October."

"Why?"

"Because the hospital is nearly empty then." Helene chuckled at my mystification. "You know how it is in the homeland—patients all want to be at home for Christmas; and the doctors want to enjoy the holidays, so they cooperate and allow all but the very ill to be discharged."

"Yes, but you said October, not December."

"Of course. India is not a Christian country; so they don't observe Christmas like we do. Their big holiday season is around October when they have the *pujas,* or worship seasons, for their special deities. They celebrate in much the same manner as we do at Christmastime. Since all the patients want to be at home with their families, no one comes into the hospital unless it is absolutely necessary."

Chapter 6

Caesarean Birth

"If we were working in a village and someone called you to assist with a birth, would you know what to do?" My husband's question came at me like a bolt from the blue.

"Of course not. I trained as a secretary, not a nurse."

"Then you ought to learn. Why don't you ask Dr. Evelyn or Helene to let you see some deliveries?"

I did not relish the idea, but knowing that he was right, I arranged with Helene to send me word next time a baby was due in daylight hours, and I would come up to the hospital and learn what I could.

Two weeks went by, and no messenger came. Hardly believing that no babies had been born at the hospital during that time, I made inquiries—sure enough, in the bustle of hospital life she had forgotten my request.

Four days later I was busy superintending my children's school lessons when Helene's mali arrived with a note: "A village woman is in labor. Come quickly."

Since David was away in the car, I hastily commandeered a bicycle, threw last-minute instructions over my shoulder, and sped off. Pedaling furiously, I reached the hospital in ten minutes, only to be met at the door by an apologetic nurse; the woman had given birth to a son only minutes after the mali had left on his errand.

A week later the whole experience was repeated,

except that this time the baby was a girl, and I began to lose my zeal for lessons in village midwifery.

To cheer me, Dr. Evelyn said that she had a Caesarean operation scheduled for the next day and I could come and watch that. But I panted up to the hospital at the appointed time only to discover that the operation had been postponed. The patient had been in labor for three days and had a previous history of two dead babies and one Caesarean birth, but she was still crying and pleading to have this baby normally.

Dr. Evelyn sighed as she explained her stubbornness. "All her village friends have their babies without operations, and she can't understand why her case is different. I've tried to explain to her she has a peculiar pelvic structure that prevents normal delivery. I'll just have to leave her until she gets so tired of the pain that she asks for a 'Caesar' or until her husband insists. Fortunately the fetal heart is still very strong."

I knew the patient slightly because she was the wife of one of our ministerial workers. Despite the fact that she had a middle-school education, prejudice and custom ruled, and "book learning" was something that did not apply to daily living.

As if she read my thoughts, Dr. Evelyn nodded. "Since she's had one successful Caesarean, I don't understand why the poor woman is so frightened. I'll speak to her husband when he visits her tonight. Come up at the same time tomorrow in case he says to go ahead with it."

When I arrived at the outer surgery door next morning, Dr. Evelyn signaled me to come in. "We're doing it this morning. You'll find a spare gown and mask in my dressing room. Hurry! They'll be bringing her in at any minute."

I hurried and was back in the theater in time to see

37

them lift the sleeping woman onto the operating table. The anesthetist took up his position at her head, and the group bowed their heads reverently while Dr. Neale offered prayer.

I stood on a footstool behind Dr. Evelyn so that I could see without being in anyone's way. From the instrument tray at her side she selected a scalpel. Its tiny size amazed me. I don't suppose I expected doctors to use carving knives, but this little instrument did not look as if it could cut anything.

Because it was the patient's second Caesarean, Dr. Evelyn began by cutting out the long, thin strip of old scar tissue and discarding it. Then she began to cut more deeply. I could not see much of the wound because sterile towels protected the area and countless gloved hands seemed to be moving up and down mechanically—cutting, mopping, tying, mopping.

From somewhere a housefly came buzzing around Dr. Neale's head, and Helene called my name and nodded toward a flyswatter setting in lonely state upon a tall white stool. I got down and chased the insect until it settled for a lucky instant (for me) on a nurse's back.

I watched again. Suddenly the doctor reached the womb, and the amniotic waters poured out, flooding the cavity. An Indian nurse hurriedly pushed forward a machine and inserted a long tube with a nozzle at the end of it into the wound. The machine sucked and gurgled as water, blood, and mucus drained out into a glass jar.

Flat metal hooks held the incision open. With Helene retracting on one side and Dr. Neale on the other, they stretched the wound to capacity. Even so, it looked to me like an awfully small opening out of which to take a full-term baby, and I watched fascinated as Dr. Evelyn's gloved hands maneuvered the fetus. A small, shell-like something showed palely through the mess. Was it the baby's ear?

Surely the doctor was having difficulty. Her hands could not get inside to take a firm grip on the slippery little form. Why didn't she make the incision bigger? I began to sweat with anxiety, and my mask got in my mouth as I bit my lips.

Again the doctor's hands moved this way and that while the others strained on the opening. No one spoke. The atmosphere was hot and tense. I thought of my baby at home.

"O God," I prayed silently, "save this woman's child." For an instant tears blinded me, but I blinked them furiously away as I saw Dr. Evelyn get her grip. In a moment the baby's head was out. A skillful twist, a faint sucking sound, and the body was free. With her left hand she held the blue-white mite by the heels and wiped mucus from its mouth with her right forefinger. The infant gasped and gave a feeble cry. The cord was cut, and the baby was handed over to Helene.

When the placenta was detached, the tedious task of sewing up the womb began, and after that the muscle, fat, skin. Layer after layer of slow stitching that took more time than the operation.

Mother instinct sent me sneaking into the next room to admire the baby. But in there all was not well. Helene's face was red with tension and exertion as she worked over him. Dishes of water stood on the table, and she plunged the infant into hot water, then cold, hot, cold. Then—he gasped but did not breathe. An Indian nurse pumped the baby's legs rhythmically while Helene replaced her mask and breathed into his mouth. There was no flicker of life. I wrung my hands in helpless anguish.

"Get some ice. Is there any more hot water?" I ran to see. The freezing chamber of the refrigerator was a solid block of ice. Some underling had neglected to defrost it. Frantically I clawed and pushed and prayed, and finally a tray of cubes snapped free. The hot-water kettle was empty, but a pan full of instruments had just been boiled on the Primus. I emptied the water off them into a dish, and the plunging began again. Hot . . . cold . . . hot . . . cold. "Breathe, baby," Helene commanded desperately as she worked on the limp blue form. She pressed his diminutive chest and forced air from her mouth into his lungs.

Hours passed—in reality minutes—and at last the baby began to lose his unearthly pale color and turn a dull red. The nurses redoubled their efforts, and the wrinkled little face screwed into a thin cry. Triumphantly Helene held him up by his heels and gave him a hearty slap. The baby screamed indignantly.

Trembling with relief, I went back into the surgery. Dr. Evelyn did not raise her eyes from her stitching, but her bent back was a question mark.

"Yes," I said. "The baby's all right—now."

Chapter 7

Hope for the Hopeless

I knew her as "Chandra's wife," but some of the villagers called her "Basu's mother," for it is not Indian etiquette to call a woman by her given name after she is married.

Chandra and his wife had been married for about twelve years and had five children, but one by one three of them died. Yesterday the fourth, little Sushila, had taken suddenly ill and within hours had been carried off, silent and still, to the burning ghat.

Chandra's wife threw the end of her sari over her head and wailed piteously. Why had this happened? What had she done to offend the gods that they should snatch her children away like this? Wasn't she an honest, hardworking woman who always minded her own business and kept out of trouble? Didn't she join Chandra in offering sacrifices to the gods before rice-planting and at puja times? Then why had four of their children died? It was too much. Chandra's wife wailed and wept until she fell exhausted to the floor.

Skinny little Basu, crouching near the door of the hut, watched his mother and wondered when she would stop crying and cook rice for the evening meal. He was hungry. Father would soon come in from the fields, and he would be hungry too.

For a long time Basu watched and waited while his mother wept. The shadows lengthened, and inside the hut it became dark and frightening. Sniveling a little, he shuffled across the room and curled up on the floor beside her.

41

When Chandra came in, he found them huddled together in a corner asleep. Another husband would probably have callously kicked his wife awake with a bare foot and ordered her to prepare his meal, but Chandra was not like that.

Quietly he put down his hoe, and going to a secret place in the cracks between the shrunken mud-brick walls, he found a small coin. Slipping down to the village tea shop, he bought a glass of steaming tea and a thin, dry cracker. It wasn't much to fill the stomach of a hungry working man, but like many of the villagers he was used to being hungry most of the time.

Chandra sipped his tea and made it last as long as he could. He drew his knees up and moodily rested his head on his crossed arms as he sat on the wooden bench. He wondered what he had done that the gods should bring upon him so many curses—drought, flood, poverty, death. Why? Why?

Abruptly Chandra decided to visit his friend Bissewar—he might know the answer. All the villagers regarded Bissewar as a wise man because he had attended school, and they trusted him to write their few letters for them and to take care of their even fewer business deals. Bissewar had traveled too—he had been to the city many times; and when the mood took him, he could hold his listeners enthralled for hours with his tales of the wonders he had seen.

Chandra walked down the dusty street, pushed aside the tattered curtain that hung across the doorway, and walked inside. He did not knock or call out to announce his arrival. According to village custom he simply went in. Bissewar looked up from the book he was reading and nodded gravely.

"Basu's mother is well?" he asked as Chandra seated himself cross-legged on the floor.

"Her body is well but her heart is sick." Chandra's voice was toneless.

42

Bissewar nodded. "Medicine can cure a sick body, but only time can heal a sad heart." And then in answer to the unspoken question in Chandra's eyes he said slowly, "Only the gods know why these things happen, and they do not tell."

For a long time the men sat in silence, and then Chandra left as abruptly as he had come. He did not bid his friend good night, he did not make excuses; he simply left when he felt like going.

Chandra's wife and child still lay in the corner of the room, and he took care not to disturb them as he unrolled a straw mat in the center of the hut, pulled a thin cloth over his head to foil the mosquitos, and fell asleep.

Daylight brought no relief to their sad hearts, and after her husband and son had gone to work in the fields, Chandra's wife listlessly began her household tasks. She used a bundle of leaves to sweep the dirt floor of the hut and dragged her unwilling feet to the village well to draw water and carry it back in a huge earthenware pot balanced on her head. Squatting beside the ditch, she washed clothes by pounding them hard with a short, thick stick. At dusk she prepared a scanty meal of boiled rice and a thin, fiery curry of chili and onion.

Chandra and Basu cleared every grain of rice from their enamel plates and sighed contentedly as they licked their fingers. But Chandra's wife ate nothing. "The light of my life has gone out," she muttered. "Let me also die."

Days crawled by, each longer and sadder than the last, and still Chandra's wife refused to eat. Occasionally a neighbor woman persuaded her to drink a little tea and eat a mouthful of chapati, but it was scarcely enough to keep a bird alive, and soon she became too weak to work, too weak even to walk. Her flesh melted away until she became nothing more than a staring-eyed skeleton with dry, cracked skin stretched over her bones.

The villagers gathered in little groups and whispered and nodded among themselves. It was only a matter of time, they agreed, and Chandra's wife would join her four children.

Chandra saw their looks and nods and knew what they were saying. But what could he do? In his simple way he loved his wife, and he did not want her to die. He pondered the problem and then decided to visit Bissewar again.

As before, he pushed aside the tattered curtain that hung across the doorway and entered unannounced. Bissewar looked up. The spectacles perched on the end of his nose gave him an owlish appearance in keeping with his reputation for wisdom. He waited until Chandra sat cross-legged on the earth floor and then said, "Basu's mother is sick?" The tone of his voice made the words a question.

"Unto death." Chandra's shoulders sagged, and his voice was flat and hopeless.

For long minutes they sat in silence. Then Bissewar said, "There are many government hospitals to cure sicknesses, but they are crowded and understaffed, and rich patients get the best attention. But down near the city there is a mission hospital directed by white missionaries. They care for sick bodies and offer healing for the heart as well."

"Near the city?" echoed Chandra. That was a hundred miles away, and how could a poor man like him afford to travel so far? Many other husbands would have shrugged and dismissed the idea—wives were easy enough to come by, and one woman could work as well as another—but not Chandra. His thoughts tumbled and jumbled together as he listened to Bissewar droning on, extolling the virtues of the little hospital.

44

"You pay as you are able; no one is turned away. If they don't know what to do, they call upon their God for help. They are very kind and even give their own blood to save a life. I swear it is true. If Basu's mother can be healed, they will do it."

Chandra nodded and unfolded his skinny legs. All the way home he pondered what Bissewar had told him. But how could he take his wife there? He had no money and no valuables that he could sell. The only thing in the world that he owned was his plow-bullock. Perhaps he could borrow money on that?

A week later Dr. Evelyn told me the story and took me into the ward to see Chandra's wife. As she felt for the woman's wavering pulse, I marveled that the spark of life still flickered in such an emaciated body. Her skin wrinkled and puckered over her fleshless bones; her voice was so weak that Dr. Evelyn had to bend low to catch her faint whisper; but there was hope in her sunken eyes, and I wondered what had awakened the will to live. Was it the gentle touch of the dedicated white hand patting her thin shoulder, or was it the hospital atmosphere hallowed by the presence of God-fearing workers?

Dr. Evelyn lifted the sick woman's head and held a glass of milk to her pallid lips. Then I saw something that I had not noticed when we entered: the same shiny, copper-bottomed American saucepan that I had seen in the doctors' kitchen stood on the bedside locker.

I felt as wise as Bissewar as I nodded to myself. I knew what had changed Chandra's wife. It was caring personified in her husband's solicitude, the gentle touch, the loving atmosphere—and the nourishment provided by the doctors' cows, which were as much a part of the hospital's lifesaving equipment as the X-ray machine or the operating theater.

45

Chapter 8

Romance

When Vasanti came to work at the hospital, we thought we had never seen a smaller nurse with a bigger smile. One only had to say, "Good morning, Vasanti," to be dazzled by its brightness. The girl's elfish brown face lit up like an Aladdin lamp, and she giggled captivatingly as she returned the greeting.

But there was nothing inane about Vasanti. Quite the contrary. She was a fully trained nurse and a good one—all four feet eleven and a half inches of her, and it was with dismay that Helene heard by way of the hospital grapevine that Vasanti was soon to be married.

"Whom is she marrying? She's a wonderful nurse, and I don't want to lose her. Is it someone local? One of the male nurses?"

"No, she's going to marry Sumer, Mrs. Chand's brother."

"Mrs. Chand's brother? But Mrs. Chand comes from North India and Vasanti is from the South—that's a thousand miles apart. How did they ever meet each other?"

"Oh, they haven't met each other at all."

Helene's mouth set in a firm line of disapproval. She had heard of the custom of marriage being arranged by a go-between who settled everything according to the parents' wishes, with the couple concerned not being consulted at all. But among the Christians she thought there was usually a suspicion of romance. Either the couple came from the same

locality, they had met at school, their parents or sib-
lings were known to each other, or there was some
vague connecting link of sorts, but this arrangement
appeared totally devoid of any humane aspect.

Underneath Helene's stern exterior beat the ten-
derest, most sentimental of hearts, and the idea of
marriage without love was distasteful to her. Finally,
however, curiosity overcame her, and she continued
to question the junior nurse who had brought the
news until, little by little, she learned the whole story.

The eldest of a family of seven girls and one lone
boy, Mrs. Chand was devoted to her young brother. In
typical Eastern fashion in which the whole family
sticks together even after they are grown up and married, she helped the lad through school and college by
paying part of his fees and supplying clothes and
pocket money. When their parents died, she assumed
full responsibility for the youth. Now that he was
working as a ministerial intern, she considered it was
time that he married.

Mrs. Chand had eyed all the single girls at the
hospital, but for varying reasons they had not qual-
ified as prospective sisters-in-law. Either they were
already betrothed, they were not pretty enough, or she
had something else against them. But when Vasanti
arrived on the scene, Mrs. Chand felt that she had
found the answer.

Vasanti's cute little face and dancing brown eyes
were sufficiently close to Mrs. Chand's ideas of
beauty to meet with her approval. Her dainty figure
and tiny, capable hands were evidently to Mrs.
Chand's liking. The fact that she had matriculated
from high school and done four years of training to
become a graduate nurse made her stakes high on the
marriage market where educated girls are much
sought after. Vasanti had other bonuses in Mrs.
Chand's eyes also—a Christian of the same religion as

her brother, ability to sing sweetly, an only child (which meant that a prospective husband would not be called upon in later years to help support a host of brothers- and sisters-in-law). Mrs. Chand lost no time in writing to her brother and telling him about her find.

The reply came promptly. "She sounds all right. Go ahead and make all the arrangements, and I will marry her."

So Mrs. Chand wrote to Vasanti's father and extolled the virtues of her only brother and his need for a good wife. She carefully listed his past accomplishments, his present progress, and his future prospects.

Vasanti's father, being a doting daddy and a man wise in the ways of the world, and of go-betweens in particular, made diligent inquiries from the young man's former teachers and associates, his present employers and friends, and ascertained for himself whether the young man was as blameless and his prospects as bright as they were purported to be.

Having done all this, Vasanti's father came to the conclusion that Sumer would, indeed, be a suitable match for his daughter, and wedding arrangements were proceeding.

"But what about Vasanti?" protested Helene with a distressed expression on her light-complexioned, Western face. "Doesn't she deserve any say in the matter? What if she doesn't like the looks of him when she sees him?"

"She will do as her father tells her." The junior nurse shrugged and went off to the wards to make beds.

Helene sat primly at her desk, drumming her fingers on its white-painted surface. She was scandalized at the idea of that "darling girl" being forced to marry someone whom she had never seen and whom she might not like when she did see him. She thought long, dark thoughts about the absence of that intrinsic quality called *love* and wondered how the marriage could possibly be happy without it.

She pondered the possibility of talking to Nurse Chand and urging her to send for her brother immediately so that he and Vasanti would have a chance to become acquainted with each other before they met at the altar.

Or would it be better to talk to Vasanti herself and extract a promise that she would refuse to marry the man unless she felt that she could learn to love him? After all, if her father loved her, he wouldn't really force her into a disagreeable marriage, would he?

All sorts of other possibilities ran through her mind, but in the end she stopped drumming her fingers on the desk and sighed a deep sigh that seemed to come right up from the soles of her sensible nursing shoes, and decided that she had better not interfere at all. This was the way that marriages had been arranged for centuries—perhaps millennia—past, and it might be wiser to let custom run its course.

All the same, she promised herself, she would pray extra hard for the darling girl and hope that by some miracle of God the marriage would be a happy one.

Several days before the wedding date Sumer arrived to stay with Mrs. Chand, and Helene's fears were somewhat allayed when he was brought around to meet her and to woo her approval. Sumer, sporting a fashionable little "toothbrush"-sized moustache and wearing a wide smile that almost rivaled Vasanti's, proved to be quite a personable young man, tall and dapper. He spoke impeccable English, and the expression that softened his manly face when he spoke about marrying *that girl*, made Helene's own heart flutter sympathetically.

Yes—she smiled as she watched Sumer being

49

shepherded off to meet his bride-to-be—Cupid is Cupid after all, and if in the East he aims his darts in a different manner from his Western counterpart, who was she to say whether the outcome was better or worse?

Chapter 9

The Slayer of the Innocent

Narain's wife had borne a daughter. The proud grandmother sat on the ground outside the hut with the newborn babe lying across her bare feet while she washed its tiny body.

The weak, early-morning sun did little to dispel the bleakness of the wind, and the baby mewled helplessly as the scrap of rag dipped in cold water was rubbed roughly over her little back. Grandmother was trying to scrub off the waxy white substance that often adheres to the newborn and did not know that a gentle rub with oil would easily have cleaned the mite. She did not know, either, that exposing the unclothed infant to cold water and piercing wind risked its death.

Pale and exhausted from her recent delivery, Narain's wife lay on the bare earth floor inside the hut. She did not know that the risk of infection in her unhygienic surroundings was terrifyingly great. The umbilical cord had been cut with the only knife the household possessed—a huge curved blade also used for chopping firewood, cutting grass, or killing snakes. The cord had been tied with a shred of jute soaked in water from the village dam where buffalo wallowed, men bathed, and women did the family wash.

Miraculously Narain's wife and baby survived the ordeal of birth. Many relatives assisted in rearing the infant. They provided her with a silver charm to protect her from evil and used a black string to bind it around her fat little stomach. They kept her small round head closely shaved to prevent her from catching cold. When her teeth began to trouble her, there was no lack of grimy fingers to rub the aching, inflamed gums.

Fed only on her mother's milk, the baby flourished until eight or nine months old, then she became fretful and grew thin and pale. The relatives accepted this as normal behavior and took no notice except to hand her around from one to another to dandle and pat and try to distract her ceaseless wails by constant movement.

Then the baby erupted in boils. The relatives, nodding wisely, told the young mother that her milk was too rich for the child and she would have to eat less.

The unfortunate mother, already anemic and undernourished, obediently ate less. There was no one there to tell her that the baby was hungry and that her diminishing milk supply and the baby's pearly teeth were signals that the child should be given solid food.

For several months the baby grew thinner and weaker. Her hair fell out, and she could not sit up alone, much less creep or walk. When she contracted dysentery, the worried relatives began trying their native remedies. But nothing did any good, and the disease quickly completed the work of reducing the baby, already in a weakened state, to a skin-covered skeleton.

Now the maternal grandmother wailed as if the child were already dead. The aunts and uncles conferred in voluble groups. A few held the opinion that something more ought to be done, but the majority insisted that the child was as good as dead now, so why spend hard-earned money on her when Narain's wife would be sure to bear another child next year? The baby's youthful parents, confused and helpless, listened to the talk as they gazed in anguish at the dying child. Finally it was decided that as one of the brothers-in-law had to go next day to see the local doctor, Narain and his wife might as well go along, too, and take the child to the doctor.

But the doctor took one quick look at the child and hustled the group out of his office. "Go to the mission hospital," he shouted.

Dr. Evelyn winced when she examined the suffering mite. It seemed impossible that the incredibly dirty and emaciated baby could survive. But food, medicine, and warm baths—together with lots of love and prayers—might bring about a miracle.

A few days later I chanced to visit the hospital, and Dr. Evelyn took me in to see the baby. "The poor little thing was in a bad way when they brought her in, and"—she interrupted herself to pull down the sheet—"see how thin she still is."

I looked and gasped and looked again. Here in the bed one of those heartrending United Nations appeal photographs of starving children came to life. Here was the same large head and shrunken face, the sparse hair, the sunken eyes, and at the end of bony arms the same clawlike fingers clutching feebly at nothing.

Dr. Evelyn drew back the covers farther, and I had to turn away to hide my horror. Every bone in the little one's body stood out as clearly as if no skin covered it at all.

"Is there any hope for her?"

"I think so. It is too soon to be certain yet. When they brought her in, she was still able to suck quite strongly, but the mother has scarcely any milk. We put the baby on formula and vitamins, and to give her a good start in her fight for life I gave her some blood as soon as she came in."

"It's no wonder you are so pale," I rebuked. Evelyn had collapsed twice in the past few weeks, and we lost

53

no opportunity to point out that she could do a lot more good by taking care of her health and being a live doctor than by giving one transfusion too many and becoming a memorial plaque.

"But you don't understand," she defended.

I sighed. I understood only too well what she meant. If she asked the relatives of the baby to give blood, they would either refuse point-blank or else readily agree to give it "tomorrow" and then disappear. If she did manage to find a paid blood donor, then one of the relatives would plead that it was not an auspicious day, and the next day there would be some other excuse, and so it would go on. But if she went ahead and gave the transfusion without the relatives knowing anything about it, then in most cases the patients lived.

"But why does it always seem to be you who gives the blood?" I argued.

"Because I'm always the nearest donor, and I'm a universal blood type. We would lose precious time if we tried to find anyone else." Evelyn smiled at my worry. "You'd do the same. It only takes a little."

I gave a helpless shrug. How many "littles" of blood had been drawn from her veins and transfused into the bodies of her dying brown-skinned sisters and brothers, only the angels in heaven knew.

I kept in close contact with "Starvation Picture," as I nicknamed the baby, and within days I could see that she had taken a turn for the better. Evelyn said it would take a long time, but with good food and proper care the baby would certainly survive.

Three weeks passed and Starvation Picture had put on some weight and showed definite signs of improvement, when the relatives appeared at the hospital. They had come to take the baby and her mother back to the village for the annual pujas.

"But the baby will die if you take her away from

the hospital now," Dr. Evelyn protested. "Can't you see that because of our treatment she is looking ever so much better?"

"They must be back in the village for the pujas; it is our custom."

"Take the mother along, but let the baby stay here," Helene added her plea.

The relatives turned a deaf ear and stubbornly began to collect the mother's few belongings together. In a last desperate hope that they might listen to the advice of their own countrymen, Helene called two of the Indian senior nurses to reason with the relatives. But it proved useless. They stood with Dr. Evelyn and Helene and watched with helpless frustration as the relatives carried little "Starvation" off to her doom.

Evelyn's shoulders sagged slightly, and her eyes glistened with tears as she turned to Helene. "Well, we saved her life, but she will be in the same state of starvation and neglect within days of reaching home. They promised to bring her back next month when the pujas are over, but I know they won't, and I doubt that she will live that long anyway."

Helene nodded and voiced the dream that all the medical workers shared: "We need a whole army of workers to go from village to village and house to house teaching these poor people the rudiments of hygiene and baby care so that situations like this can be prevented."

Chapter 10

The Convert

Sunderlal was sick. Pain distorted his ordinarily pleasant face, and his tall frame daily grew more stooped and gaunt. Once he trudged eight miles to see a doctor at the nearest public hospital and sat for hours in the busy waiting room watching other patients come and go. Some who arrived much later than he received attention and went their way, but still he waited.

Dully he noticed that those who received quick service had given money to the man sitting at the outside desk taking down the names and particulars of the patients. He wondered why they paid him; this was a government hospital, and treatment was free. In his innocence he did not realize that these people were buying first place in the line.

When at last Sunderlal's turn came, the doctor was tired and irritable. Finding that Sunderlal had no money to pay for expensive injections, he angrily waved him away. "Charity beds are all filled, and there's a waiting list a mile long. Come back in six weeks, and we'll see what can be done."

Hastily scribbling a prescription on a scrap of paper, he handed it to an orderly who beckoned Sunderlal to follow him to the dispensary, where another long line of patients drooped against the whitewashed walls. If only Sunderlal had known and if only he had the money, a little baksheesh would place his name high on the list of those needing free inpatient care or it would buy him first place in the line waiting for medicine at the dispensary window.

But Sunderlal did not know, and Sunderlal was poor—as most villagers are. Very few know with certainty where next week's food will come from, and some do not even know whether they will eat tomorrow.

Sunderlal and his wife, thrifty hardworking farmers, usually managed to have some rice in their bins and a few chilis drying on the roof of their small hut. But now with Sunderlal too sick to work his fields, things looked hopeless. His thin little wisp of a wife spent so much time caring for him that she could not do much in the field. Her sad brown eyes grew sadder and more worried as she watched her husband grow weaker and the level of rice in the bins get lower. What would become of them?

Weeks lengthened into months, and their story would have ended unhappily if Mandhu had not happened along. Mandhu, Sunderlal's progressive young nephew, owned a bicycle and a wristwatch, and he wore European-style trousers. Because he worked as a clerk in a city store, he seemed, to his simple village relatives, to know everything.

When Mandhu breezed in and heard the sorry story of his uncle's long illness and of the doctor's indifference, he snapped his fingers and exclaimed, "I know the very place for you, Uncle. There's a small mission hospital not far from my home village, with two white doctors who treat everyone the same. Rich or poor, it makes no difference; one doesn't have to give baksheesh to get treatment there."

Sunderlal shook his head. "No doctor-sahib would do that; they grow rich by their fees."

Mandhu grunted impatiently. "It's true, I tell you. My own mother's cousin-sister's niece was there, and I heard it from her lips. She was three weeks in the hospital before she was cured, and she had plenty of time to observe the foreigners very closely."

Sunderlal's wife clicked her tongue in wonder. "Why are they different?"

"I don't know. Not all foreigners act like that. . . . I've had much experience." Mandhu spat out a mouthful of red betel-nut juice and continued thoughtfully, "Perhaps it is their religion. They all follow Jesus Christ, and every morning they say prayers before they begin work. Mother's cousin-sister's niece said they pray over the sick ones, and they recover. If you want to get better, I advise you to go there."

Without another word Mandhu rose from his stool, smoothed down the crease of his trousers, ran a comb through his oily black hair, and went on his way.

Sunderlal closed his eyes and lay back on his bamboo cot. His wife squatted quietly on the mud floor, motionless, thinking. Suddenly she leaped up and darted to the darkest corner of the hut, her reaching fingers searching about in the thatched roof until they closed on a small rag bundle. Tugging it open she began to count out the grubby bank notes, unrolling each one carefully and spreading it out on the ground beside her husband's pallet—seven precious pieces of paper—one large and six small—sixteen rupees in all.

Sunderlal opened his tired eyes and looked at her. "The train fare would be eleven rupees," he said in flat, despairing tones.

His wife's birdlike face brightened with hope. "Yes, but we could take our own food with us, rice and chilis and onions. And Nephew said that those who cannot pay fees are not turned away. It is our last chance. You must get well again."

Sunderlal turned his face to the wall and groaned in misery, "I'll never be well again."

58

But in the end they went to the hospital and found it just as Mandhu had said. They explained to the man at the registration desk that they had no money left—the last of their savings had been used for the train fares. He nodded and handed them a blue card that said *charity* in English letters, though they couldn't read the word.

When Sunderlal's turn came, Dr. Neale asked many questions, examined him thoroughly, and then patted his thin shoulder. "Poor fellow, you've suffered a lot, but we can help you. An operation is necessary, but it's not a serious one, and in a week or two you'll be as good as new."

The male nurse translated this to Sunderlal, and he was incredulous but joyful. With typical village gratitude he stooped and touched the doctor's feet and tremulously salaamed everyone in the doctor's office before stumbling outside, murmuring over and over, "Mandhu was right; he was right. They can make me well."

As Sunderlal lay in his bed recovering from his operation he decided to find out why the people at this hospital were so kind. He talked to the nurses, the other patients, the servants. He asked questions, many questions, and thought the answers over carefully. At last he came to a conclusion.

"It must be their religion," he told his wife. "I've found out that these nurses and orderlies get less salary than they would at a government hospital. Even the white doctors are not rich. Yet no one asks for baksheesh. No one grumbles. They are always happy and willing to help the patients. Yes, I'm sure it *is* their Jesus that makes them different. I must find out more."

Next morning as Nurse Jacob dressed his wound Sunderlal plied him with questions about his religion.

59

"Which gods do you worship? What offerings do you have to make to please them? Do your gods love Indians as well as white men?"

Nurse Jacob answered his questions, but other patients were waiting for him, and he had to hurry on with his work. "Can you read? I'll get you some tracts that will tell you more."

Yes, Sunderlal could read a little Hindi. But by the time he laboriously spelled out the words, he did not understand much of what he read. So when Nurse Jacob got off duty in the afternoon, he came back and explained the gospel story to him. Sunderlal drank it in as thirstily as sand drinks water.

Sunderlal's wound healed well. A week later he was discharged, but he was reluctant to leave while learning so much. He talked it over with his wife and Nurse Jacob. Together they decided that his wife should return to the village and do what she could in the field but that he would stay awhile in Nurse Jacob's house and learn more.

Night after night the faithful Indian nurse took out his Bible and read to Sunderlal and answered his many questions. And as Sunderlal listened to the wonderful story of salvation the words of love sank deep into his heart as well as his brain, and he decided that he must become a follower of Jesus.

As he prepared to go home and tell his wife and his village friends all that he had learned, he thought how happy they would be to see him well again and to hear the wonderful news of Christ's salvation, free to all men.

For several months nothing was heard of Sunderlal or his wife, and the hospital staff wondered what had happened to them. Then suddenly they were back again. They told a sad but not uncommon tale of ridicule, persecution, and boycott that finally drove them to leave their village home and seek peace at the only haven they knew—the little mission hospital.

Nurse Jacob, the doctors, and the rest of the staff rejoiced that Sunderlal and his wife had stood the test and remained true to their faith in Jesus, but their return to the hospital presented problems. It was one thing to give free lodging and treatment to the sick, even to provide them with food if necessary; but it was quite another to provide food and lodging for well persons. If the hospital started doing that, there would be no end—people for miles around would give up working and flock to such a sanctuary.

Very tactfully Dr. Neale explained the matter to Sunderlal. The hospital compound, already filled to capacity—Sunderlal could see that for himself—had no place. Was it actually impossible for him to stay on at his village? Was his life really in danger? Didn't he have relatives anywhere else with whom he could live?

No. No. Sunderlal wanted no charity. To everyone's relief he had the solution himself. He knew what to do—just give him permission to start a small business near the hospital gate, and he and his wife would look after themselves.

Permission was gladly given, and they set to work. With a sheet of tin from here and a few boards dragged from there, in no time Sunderlal and his wife had thrown together a shack on the side of the road outside the hospital's big double gates.

Then they set up shop. Their first stock consisted of a small pile of coal and a dozen sticks of wood. During his stay in the hospital Sunderlal had noticed how difficult it was for the relatives to procure fuel for the tiny stoves. Some wandered miles into the jungle searching for sticks and bark, and others walked miles in the opposite direction and bought coal and sticks from the merchants in town; now they could procure supplies close at hand.

61

Selling the first stock, Sunderlal used the money to buy more. Within a month his handfuls of coal had grown to a sizable pile and his dozen sticks of wood had multiplied into a respectable heap.

His business continuing to prosper, Sunderlal added matches, salt, and lumps of hard brown jaggery (palm sugar) to his little store. He displayed his goods on green banana leaves spread on the dust in front of the wood and coal pile, and he or his wife sat cross-legged beside them, ready to serve their customers.

But on Sabbaths they closed the store, tied the makeshift door shut with string, and seated themselves on unaccustomed chairs inside the neat brick church that adjoined the hospital. Sunderlal, slightly deaf, set his chair right up close to the rostrum so that he would not miss a word the speaker said. His wife sat on the other side of the church along with the female nurses, wives, and children.

When it came time for the offering, Sunderlal rose solemnly from his conspicuous chair. With unconscious ostentation he delved deeply into the little cloth bag that he took from his shirt pocket and brought out two coins. He slowly crossed to the other side of the church and gave one to his wife. He carried the other back with him to his place, and when the offering plate passed along the rows, their lined faces beamed with pleasure as they dropped in their mites.

Months passed. One day we saw neat piles of bricks on the side of the road. Sunderlal stood proudly by directing the workmen, and presently a tiny, boxlike, one-room shed took shape. Now they had a real house-cum-shop, and as God prospered them they were able to buy sacks of rice for resale; also atta* and lentils and soap; yes, and sago** and *maida* to tempt the finicky appetites of the sick.

---

* Unsorted wheat flour.
** A powdery starch used for thickening.

But their faith met another test. One night Sunderlal's wife awoke to hear someone moving around in the small hut. Thinking her husband was going outside to answer nature's call, she spoke his name loudly and put out her hand to touch the dark form silhouetted against the open doorway. But her hand slid off the greased skin of a naked man, and she screamed an alarm as the thief dashed away.

The gatekeeper and the night watchman answered her cries. It was no use giving chase because everyone knew that the thieves took off their clothes and oiled their bodies so that they could easily wriggle free if they were caught. Besides, the distant thud of running feet told them that they had a good start on any pursuers.

The commotion awakened Sunderlal, who soon realized that thieves had carried off all the shop stock and all their belongings—every pot and pan and blanket. Stumbling to the farthest corner of the hut, he groped around in the little space where roof and wall met—but the small cloth bag of money was gone too—the thieves knew the usual hiding places of villagers who mistrust city banks.

With morning light, everyone knew of the calamity. They repeated the story again and again with suitable additions and embellishments. Every mobile person on the hospital compound came to see and to sympathize and to hear from the couple's own lips the account of the nighttime devastation.

The doctors came, too, and Helene and the nearby missionaries, and after they left, they held a little consultation in Dr. Neale's office. Between them they contributed enough money to set Sunderlal up in business again—this time with a stout chain and padlock to fasten his door at night. Once more—by dint of hard work, strict economy, and the blessing of God—the little shop prospered.

63

Chapter 11

Brother Joshua

Dr. Neale laid down his pen and handed the prescription to the waiting patient. The man took it in his cupped hands, raised them to his forehead in respectful salute, and shuffled off to present the precious paper at the dispensary window.

"Next, please." Dr. Neale adjusted his stethoscope and turned to an elderly man who edged forward and slid into the chair in front of his desk. But before he could begin asking the man his symptoms, an orderly pushed urgently through the curtained doorway.

"Doctor-sahib, two men have come from Banipur village. They want you to come quickly. Their uncle is desperately ill."

Motioning the elderly patient to wait, Dr. Neale thrust his chair back and jumped to his feet. "All right, Prem. Bring them in. Ask them what's wrong. We need to have some idea what to take with us."

For the next few moments questions and answers flew back and forth in a jumble of Hindi and local dialect, and Prem relayed in English the scraps of information he received.

"He's vomiting almost constantly. Can't even keep water in his stomach. Having frequent loose stools. Took ill very suddenly. He's so weak now they think he's dying."

"It sounds like cholera," Dr. Neale nodded. "This is the season for it—so many flies around and uncovered food sold in the bazaars. Where's Joshua? He can do anything I could do for the poor man."

64

"Perhaps he's in the lab?" Prem raised his eyebrows and shrugged. He knew as well as Dr. Neale did that Joshua could be anywhere. Joshua was a trained nurse who had taken a laboratory course. In the hospital staff book he was officially listed as "laboratory technician," but Joshua did much more than either nursing duties or peering through a microscope. When the pharmacist unexpectedly left the hospital, Joshua filled the breach, running back and forth between laboratory and pharmacy, dispensing pills and medicines in between taking blood samples and making tests.

In the operating theater, more often than not, Joshua had to act as anesthetist—and an excellent one he was. Whenever an X ray was needed, Joshua was the one who donned a leather apron and operated the X-ray machine. If a difficult intravenous injection had to be given, the nurses called for Brother Joshua— they said he could always find a vein when nobody else could do it. Joshua would be just the man to care for this cholera case.

"See if you can find him, Prem." Dr. Neale turned back to his patients.

The orderly hurried off in search of Joshua and eventually tracked him down in the boxlike darkroom where he was developing an X-ray negative. But by the time the two of them returned to Dr. Neale's office, the village messengers had disappeared.

"They've probably gone back to the village to tell their uncle that we're coming," Dr. Neale guessed, but in actual fact the opposite was true. After waiting awhile, the messengers had concluded that the search for Joshua was proving fruitless and had hurriedly caught the rickety bus into town to call another doctor. By the time Brother Joshua and Prem had collected bottles of normal saline and rubber tubing and intravenous needles and had trudged in the hot sun across the paddy fields to Banipur village, a taxi from town sped past them and stopped a few yards ahead at the sick man's house.

As the dust settled and Joshua and Prem saw a town doctor hurrying into the house they halted respectfully, uncertain whether to return to the hospital or wait awhile. Before they could make up their minds, the medico was out again. Apparently he had not inquired about the man's symptoms. Finding that the patient had cholera, he threw his hands in the air and exclaimed that he had not brought drugs suitable for treating cholera. No amount of arguments from the relatives could persuade him to touch the patient. He demanded his fee and fare and retreated to his taxi grumbling and muttering, "Stupid villagers, the man would die anyway."

Seeing Joshua and Prem armed with bottles and tubes, the doctor snorted disdainfully that his time was too valuable for that sort of thing and clambered into his taxi.

As soon as he was out of sight, the relieved relatives escorted Joshua and Prem and their paraphernalia into the house. The patient was so dehydrated that death was only hours away. While Prem hurriedly connected tubes and bottles of saline, Joshua felt for a vein in the man's arm and pushed in the needle. Soon the life-giving drip was doing its work.

At first, to save time, Prem held the bottle of saline above his head. Soon the flow was established, and Joshua directed the relatives to rig up a hook from the mosquito-net frame and suspend the bottle from it.

Every man, woman, and child of the patient's household sat or squatted on the hard earth floor carefully watching. Curious neighbors crowded the doorways or peered through the small barred windows of the little room. During the long hours that Joshua and Prem stood by to adjust the drip and make

66

sure that no one interfered with the apparatus, they had plenty of time to talk with the family and assure them that the patient would recover.

"God loves us all," Joshua explained. "He wants us to be always healthy and happy." With Prem interpreting, he began at Eden and traced the story of God's love and patience right through to the gift of His Son on the cross to save sinners.

The relatives and neighbors listened entranced. By the time the third liter bottle of saline was empty and the patient had recovered sufficiently to sit up and ask for food, Joshua was telling them about Jesus' coming back to this world again.

Joshua was like that. He was as much a missionary as any white-skinned foreigner. He and his family had left their home in the faraway south to come and work among people with different language, food habits, dress, and customs. These people sometimes resented Joshua's presence among them even more than they did the foreigners who tried to teach them new ways.

Just because Joshua had merely come from one state of his homeland to another without having traversed continents or crossed vast oceans, his parting from friends and loved ones was no less poignant. He furloughed every six years, and apart from that he depended on the postal service for contact from his home and relatives the same as every other missionary.

One day I entered the nursing office unannounced and saw Joshua and Helene bending over a tiny crib—so absorbed in what they were doing that they did not notice my presence. Finally I tiptoed over to see what they were up to.

A seriously ill baby was being given a blood transfusion, and it was Joshua who was joined by a slender tube to the mite in the cot. His blood dripped through to save the little life. I looked more closely at his arm.

The course of the large vein was pitted and scarred by the marks of many previous transfusion needles.

Again I say, Brother Joshua is as much a missionary as any of the rest of us. In paying tribute to him we also commend the countless thousands of nationals who leave their homes and loved ones to unselfishly serve the needy in their own land.

Chapter 12

Life Is Like That

The illiterate villagers keep no records of births, deaths, or marriages. The only means they have of pinpointing such events is to remember that Baba was born about the time the well ran dry in the terrible drought, or Soshi and Prem were married the year the district had a bumper rice crop, or Mamaji died three moons after the irrigation canal was opened.

So when Dr. Neale asked Shankar his age, it took some time for him and Malati his wife, arguing back and forth, to work out that he was about fifty-five. He looked more like seventy, with his wrinkled skin and thin, bent frame bearing silent witness to the hard life of the Indian peasant. Often too poor to own a bullock, he plowed his fields by drawing the crude wooden plow back and forth across the hard clods himself.

Shankar's heart was worn out by toil and hardship, and Dr. Neale could do little for him. Younger Malati was well-rounded, energetic, voluble, and touchingly devoted to her ailing husband. From his hospital bed Shankar had only to blink an eyelid, and she leaped to his side, tenderly lifting his head and giving him hot, sugary milk from a thick, chipped glass or massaging his wasted limbs with pungent mustard oil.

During the heat of the day Malati stood for hours fanning Shankar with a frayed palm leaf, putting wet rags on his head, and loosening his clothing when he gasped for breath.

Patients and staff commented on her devotion,

whispering behind her back and wondering whether she knew that her husband's case was hopeless and that the doctor was only making him more comfortable as the end approached.

At 3 AM one humid morning Shankar went to his final rest, and Malati's grief was terrifying in its intensity. As doctor drew the sheet over her husband's pallid face, she burst into agonized wails that awakened the whole hospital and brought night nurse and women patients running to comfort her.

Malati ignored them all. She beat her breast and tore at her long black hair. She threw herself onto the floor beside Shankar's bed and rolled back and forth, wailing and clawing the air in the agony of her despair.

For three hours she sobbed and wept and beat her head on the unyielding cement. Once, when another village woman squatted beside her and tried to calm her with soothing words, Malati stopped weeping and broke into a long, shrill recital of Shankar's good deeds and virtues. Then realization of her great loss overwhelmed her, and she shrieked and rolled again.

When the day staff came on duty at seven o'clock, nobody needed to tell them what had happened. They went about their duties solemn-faced and silent, their hearts wrung with pity for the weeping woman, who had no children. All her love had been centered on her husband.

At breakfast time someone brought Malati a glass of steaming tea and persuaded her to stop wailing long enough to drink it.

Noticing the silence, Helene hurried from her little office and called for one of the nurses to act as interpreter. Unpleasant as the task was, she had to discuss the disposal of Shankar's body. Hindus usually arrange for the deceased to be burned within hours of death, and Helene tried to express sympathy as she tenderly asked Malati if she wanted to take her husband's body home by taxi so that he could be cremated with full Hindu rites.

Malati's reply was a violent negative. No, she did not want that at all.

Helene tried again. Did Malati want to contact her relatives and have them come and tenderly bear the body away?

No. No, she didn't have any relatives in this district.

Then what did she want to do with her husband's body?

Malati did not know. That was the hospital's business as far as she was concerned. Shankar had died here, let the hospital take care of his body.

"Would you like to have us bury him in our little Christian cemetery?" Helene held her breath when she put that question to her. She expected that Malati would scream with fury at the suggestion of her dear one being interred in the company of Christians, even dead ones.

But Malati shrugged. "Do as you like. He's dead now." She turned her back as indication that the discussion was ended as far as she was concerned. The tea was finished, and so, it seemed, was her grief.

Helene hesitated and then decided to enlist the hospital manager's aid—surely he would know how to deal with the situation. With the nurse at her heels she hurried to Henty's office.

"But we have such a tiny plot, it's meant only for Christian burials, and there have been so many paupers lately. What will we do when there's no more space?" He spread his hands in a despairing gesture.

No one had any other solution, and finally he sighed, then consented, "All right, we'll have to help the poor woman if she has no friends or relatives. Send for the chaplain, and we'll arrange a short funeral service. Let as many as possible of the staff attend."

Helene and the nurse went back to tell Malati that her husband could be buried in the hospital's hallowed ground. "We'll have a little service for you," her voice was compassionate. "God knows all about your sorrow, and He will comfort you and care for you."

But Malati was not listening. She had already rolled threadbare blankets into a neat bundle and was stuffing the rest of her belongings into a sack.

"We can ask the man to dig the grave immediately if you are in a hurry, and the service can be held within an hour."

Malati tied her bundle with a final knot and stood up. "The bus is leaving now. My man is dead; so there's no point in my staying." She gave her nose a last wipe on the end of her sari, gathered up her bag and bundles, and marched off.

When Helene found her voice, she called after her, "There are buses leaving every hour."

Without turning around, Malati sniffed, "What's the use?" and disappeared behind the hedge at the hospital's front gate.

Helene hurried back to the manager's office. He beamed when he heard her story and realized that the hospital was now under no obligation to use up its valuable burying space.

"But what can we do with him? We can't leave a dead body lying around too long, not in this weather. Besides a new patient is already waiting for his bed."

The manager shuffled the papers on his desk and coughed uneasily. He had no answer to her logic. There was a long silence until the nurse who had been acting as interpreter suggested that the government's new medical college in town might like to have a body for the students to dissect.

The manager looked relieved and reached for the telephone. The others waited while he told his story to the heads of many departments of the college before he located the right person to deal with the situation. "Yes, indeed," the voice at the other end of the line said. The college would be very glad to have a cadaver. Messengers would be sent immediately to collect it.

So poor, unwanted Shankar was wheeled into an empty storeroom to await their arrival, and life at the hospital flowed on as usual.

As she went off duty at 6 PM, Helene passed the storeroom and gasped with dismay when she saw the silent form still lying there. "Shankar!" she exclaimed, and flew toward the manager's office.

"He's still there. In this hot weather. We must do something quickly."

The manager stared at her uncomprehendingly. His mind full of debits and credits and the nearly impossible task of balancing the hospital's budget, he had forgotten about Shankar. When she explained the new crisis to him, he looked around helplessly.

The rest of the office staff rose to the occasion. As one man the mail peon, the secretaries, the gatekeeper (who happened along at that moment), and all the bystanders who crowded into the office as soon as they became aware that something was wrong, voiced their opinions and suggestions for the disposal of the body.

Fortunately the tardy arrival of the messengers from the medical college averted the need for a decision. They arrived empty-handed and wanted to borrow a hospital cart to trundle the body back to the college.

"Nonsense. You can't wheel a hospital cart over two miles of gravel road."

The messengers were unabashed and adamant.

They would not touch the body, no, not even with the tips of their fingers. Who knew what caste the dead man might have been? Either they borrowed the cart or the body stayed where it was.

Frustrated and helpless, the staff looked at one another. But the manager knew defeat when he saw it. With an air of great resignation he gathered up his books and papers and shoved them into a drawer. Then he took out a large bunch of keys and ponderously selected one while he said in English, "It will be quicker and more face-saving if we put the body into the new ambulance and drive it down to the college for them."

And to the unconcealed delight of the messengers, he did just that.

Chapter 13

Escape From a Bear

Scarcely any rain fell that winter, and the grass withered long before the summer sun arrived to dry it out like stubble. Since the cattle had no green feed, every day Chandra and his brother, Ananda, went farther and farther from the village to cut fodder for their few miserable cows.

One hot morning found them at the outskirts of the jungle, stripping tender leaves from young saplings and tying them in bundles to carry home on their heads. Chandra, so intent on his task, failed to notice that he had wandered some distance from his brother. But even if he had noticed, he would not have worried because he knew that once the sun was high the jungle predators would be asleep in some cave or shady glen.

Only the soft swish of falling leaves and the harsh cawing of a distant crow disturbed the warm silence until Ananda's warning shout stabbed the still air like a knife:

"Bhalu! Bhalu!"

With a startled cry Chandra swung around and found himself facing a huge black bear. Before he could drop his bundle of leaves and run, the animal was upon him. Instinctively his arm jerked up to shield his face as the bear attacked. He screamed in agony as the cruel claws ripped his forearm to the bone.

There was no chance of escape. The bear's weight and the suddenness of its attack sent Chandra sprawl-

75

ing, and he lay on his back writhing and helpless as the furious creature clawed and bit.

Ananda rushed to his brother's aid, shouting and thrashing at the bear's thick hide with his stick. By some rare good fortune he managed to scare the animal off and send it lumbering back into the jungle.

Blood poured from deep cuts in Chandra's lips and chin, and his nose hung loosely on a wide swathe of flesh that flapped around his left ear when Ananda tried to sit him up. The back of his head and his forehead were gashed to the bone, and one cheek was entirely bitten off. His ears were torn, and his neck bore deep wounds, but miraculously his eyes were uninjured. He was still conscious when Ananda dragged him to his feet and half carried him to the safety of the village.

Chandra's agonized moans brought the villagers running, and they all crowded around anxiously trying to help. As they listened to the story of the attack, each one had a different theory. One said it must have been a she-bear with cubs hidden nearby. Another said it was just an ordinary grumpy bear searching for wild honey or birds' eggs. Still another pointed out that all bears are notoriously bad tempered and vicious, and any hunter will vouch for the fact that a bear doesn't need a reason before it attacks. A fourth insisted that Chandra had simply happened to get in the bear's way. But the last man was sure he had the solution. All bears, he said, are shortsighted, and this one simply mistook Chandra for another bear that was invading its territory.

Whatever the reason, here was the result. All the villagers shook their heads and wondered what to do. It was not possible for Chandra to survive such a mauling. They all agreed on that. Once again each one had a tale to tell of someone he knew who had been savaged by a bear and had died within days, even hours. No, no. It was not possible—Chandra would die—such a pity. Tsk, tsk! In the prime of life—but what to do?

"No!" Ananda shouted them down. "No, my brother must not die. He must go to a doctor."

Startled, the villagers agreed. All right. It was useless, of course—just a waste of time and money—but to please Ananda. But how? Where? Arguments and suggestions flew back and forth, and at last the village headman decided that Chandra must be taken to the mission hospital. If there was any chance of healing his dreadful wounds, the doctors there could do it.

The whole village escorted the brothers to the main road. When the ancient bus rattled into view and drew up in a cloud of dust, most of them crowded aboard to inform the driver and passengers of the accident. They shoved baskets, bundles, and people indiscriminately aside and made room for Chandra on the back seat.

Mercifully he was only half conscious during the long bumping, jolting drive to the hospital. When the bus stopped at the mission gate, most of the passengers rushed inside to tell the story so that by the time the staff had pushed a cart out to carry the injured man into surgery, a sizable crowd of staff, patients, and bystanders milled around trying to get a glimpse of him.

"It was after his brain," the hospital gatekeeper announced in sepulchral tones, rolling his black eyes and dropping his voice even lower. "Bears always crush the skull and eat the brain."

"Not the brain, the nose," a bystander contradicted. "Those gashes on his face were caused by the bear's teeth, and the ones on his head by its claws where it grasped his head in its paws and bit off his nose."

Dr. Neale was away at a conference, but Dr. Evelyn

and Helene came running when a frantic nurse brought them news of the new patient. Within minutes poor Chandra was wheeled into the operating theater.

For a moment the two women gazed helplessly at their patient. Where did one begin? Dirt, bits of stick, and dry leaves clung to the bloody mess that had been a face. The fleshy part of his nose and left cheek dangled loosely over his ear. A mass of exposed cartilage and blood took the place of his nose. He breathed painfully through his mouth and swallowed gobs of blood at every labored gasp.

"We can't give him a general anesthetic," Evelyn muttered behind her mask. "I don't see how we can use a local either, but we'll have to try. We must try to prevent his feeling pain but keep him conscious enough to cooperate, or he'll drown in his own blood."

Helene nodded, and the doctor motioned for the other helpers to gather around while she prayed for skill and guidance. Brother Joshua translated her prayer and explained to Chandra that the doctor was praying to the great God in heaven to use their skill to make him better. Even in his agony the poor fellow seemed to understand and relaxed a little.

"Will you stitch his lips and cheek while I concentrate on the nose?" Dr. Evelyn's gloved hands hovered a moment before she made the first stitch. "I really don't see how he'll ever breathe normally again. How can I sort out the air passages in this ghastly mess?"

Helene grunted a reply. She already held forceps and needle, waiting while Nelia did her best to clean Chandra's face and make it as sterile as possible. Stitching wounds was nothing new to Helene, but after all—there are wounds and *wounds*.

Minutes ticked by, marking off the hours as stitch by patient stitch the flesh was tacked into place and a mangled mess began to look like a face.

Twice during the tedious process, Chandra's nerves gave way, and with a shout and a mighty heave he burst the bands that held his arms and tossed bowls of saline and trays of sutures to the four corners of the surgery. That meant a short delay to quiet him down, gather up everything, and collect more sterile articles. But apart from these lapses, Chandra was an exemplary patient, seemingly having nerves like steel wires.

Four hours passed before Evelyn straightened her aching back and said, "Well, I think that's the last one, Helene. We must have put in scores of sutures."

Helene rubbed a gloved hand across her forehead. "I was worried about getting those on the top lip just right. I hope they don't slough, but it will be a miracle if they don't. Never in my life have I seen a person so torn about."

Evelyn nodded and slipped off her mask as she watched Joshua wheel the patient off to a private room. "We've done all we can, and the Lord will do the rest. The boy seems a healthy fellow and an outdoor type—he should pull through all right if there are no complications."

For the first few days Chandra was very ill, and the mission staff prayed earnestly for him. Every day Helene had to remove the gauze packing from his nose and repack it, a painful process that she hated as much as Chandra did. But each day as the doctors stopped at his bedside to pray and examine his stitches they went away more hopeful. No sign of infection appeared, and the patient managed to eat and sleep well. They felt sure he would recover.

Then came the great day when the sutures were taken out. Evelyn carefully clipped and pulled and exclaimed with delight, "Wonderful, the ones in the lip held long enough for the skin to join. The rest are perfectly all right. A splendid healing, and the scars will fade in time."

Dr. Neale beamed at his wife and remarked that although none of them knew what Chandra looked like before the bear attacked him, his face was nothing to be ashamed of now.

Helene came hurrying forward with a mirror, "Here, Joshua, let him look at himself, and you ask him whether he looks like he did before."

"His nose might be a little flatter than normal, but he should care as long as he can breathe properly," Dr. Evelyn commented, her smooth brow creasing into worry lines. "I did my best."

Chandra took the mirror and gazed earnestly at his reflection, then his scarred face broke into a smile, and he nodded, "Jee, ha."

All the onlookers who were gathered around his bedside broke into smiles and nodded happily to one another. Yes, he said he looked just the same.

And a little later, when the packing was taken out of his nose for the last time, Chandra gave a few preliminary snuffles and snorts and then began to breathe in normal fashion. The staff rejoiced, and Dr. Evelyn breathed a prayer of thanksgiving.

Chapter 14

The Priestess' Vow

"Madam?" The gaudy cotton curtain that served as a door into Dr. Evelyn's consulting room was drawn aside and a wizened, bearded face appeared. Imploring dark eyes fixed on her bent head as the man said hoarsely, "Madam, could you please come to visit a sick lady?"

Dr. Evelyn stopped writing the prescription and looked up. The room was filled with women patients and silent children who stared unblinkingly and listened impassively as she dealt with the patient sitting in the chair in front of her desk. As fast as one woman vacated the chair, another took her place, while outside on the wide veranda the overflow sat on benches or squatted against the wall waiting patiently for their turn to come.

Evelyn gestured toward the waiting room. "I'm sorry," she told him. "It isn't possible today. I have so many patients waiting to see me. If she is not seriously ill, couldn't you bring her here to the hospital tomorrow?"

The little dark man nodded wordlessly, and the curtain dropped back into place as he withdrew his head. Dr. Evelyn turned to the fat woman next in line. "Oh, yes, I remember you. You had a Caesarean operation. How is the baby?"

The fat woman smiled and beckoned for her mother-in-law to bring the child forward. Dr. Evelyn admired him, listened to his diminutive heartbeats, and urged his mother to have him immunized now that he was three months old. The woman nodded so emphatically that her whole body shook, "Jee, jee ha [Yes, definitely]." With more smiles and bows, that group went on their way.

A village woman with advanced tuberculosis came next. The mission hospital had no facilities for caring for infectious cases; so Evelyn took time off to run out to the nursing-office telephone and make arrangements for her to be admitted to the nearest sanatorium.

Next came a tumor, then a well-educated wealthy expectant mother, three anemias one after another, a child with hookworm, and a baby with polio. The line seemed endless.

Darkness had shrouded the compound before Dr. Evelyn tucked her stethoscope into her pocket, gave last-minute instructions at the nursing office for the care of a critically ill fever patient, and hurried home to see her own children for the first time that day.

The next day was a repetition of the one before, except that in the middle of the morning Dr. Evelyn had to take time out to deliver twins, and that put everything behind. The long lines of waiting women did not complain because of the delay—babies always come at most inconvenient times. She finished her morning clinic and went home to lunch at 3 PM. She had hardly sat down at the table when the house phone rang. Swallowing her mouthful of food, Dr. Evelyn picked up the receiver.

"There's a man here," came the muffled voice from the nursing office. "He wants you to visit a sick woman."

"I can't. I haven't done hospital rounds today. Besides, my bicycle has a puncture, and I can't do any house calls until it is mended. There are plenty of Indian lady doctors in town. Can't he go to one of them?" There was a brief pause while this message was relayed to the waiting man, and then the muffled voice continued, "He says he particularly wants you to visit her because you would understand. She is not desperately ill—he says she can wait awhile longer until you can go."

"If she is not seriously ill, then tell him to bring her out to the clinic." Evelyn put down the telephone and turned back to her cold and tasteless meal.

The next day was operating day, and work began at 7:30 AM, right after hospital worship. The doctors worked together on serious cases and dealt with minor ones alternately. First, Evelyn did a curettage, and then Neale removed a boy's tonsils. There was a heavy schedule of major surgeries, and it was past two o'clock when Dr. Evelyn removed her mask and gown and walked onto the veranda for a breath of fresh air. She almost fell over the wizened little dark man who was crouching just outside the surgery door. Scrambling to his feet, he bowed respectfully and clasped his hands in a gesture that was both supplication and greeting.

"Please, madam, will you come and see a sick lady?"

"Oh," Dr. Evelyn muttered under her breath, "the importunate widow!" She returned his polite greeting and then pointed to the long line of patients in the waiting rooms and verandas. "We are desperately busy at the hospital. Can't you possibly bring the lady out here to see me?"

The little man shook his head. "She does not leave the house, madam; she has taken a vow."

A vow. Evelyn shrugged helplessly. There were all kinds of vows. A man might give his right arm to god as an offering and hold it rigidly above his head for years until it became withered and useless. Another might take a vow of silence.

"It is absolutely impossible for me to come today,

but I'll try and visit her tomorrow if you will give me her address."

"No, madam. I shall come myself and take you to her." The little man bowed his thanks and backed away.

When Dr. Evelyn hurried out to the hospital gate at 3 PM next day, the little dark man had a taxi waiting for her. As they drove along he began to talk about the lady. She was a very devout woman who spent eight or nine hours a day in prayer, calling upon the name of her god, "Ram, Ram, Ram, Jai! Ram, Ram, Ram . . ."

Dr. Evelyn nodded. She had heard plenty of that because many patients at the hospital prayed aloud in the same manner. They never asked to be healed or made any other requests, they never gave thanks or praised their god. To them prayer simply meant repeating the god's name over and over again in wearying repetition.

"How can she have time to do this every day? Doesn't she have a husband and children to care for?"

"No, doctor-memsahib, her husband is dead, and she lives in an ashram, a holy place, at Allahabad. She is only visiting here. Nearly a year ago she made a vow before a stone image that she would devote her life to a god and would eat nothing but fruit and milk until the day of her death."

As they talked Evelyn became curious to meet this woman. Sadhus, holy men, are as prevalent in India as crows in the trees. One could not go anywhere without seeing a half-naked devotee with long matted hair and beard, body smeared with ashes or cow dung, and carrying a trident and begging bowl. They make a living by parading their piety and preying on the credulous populace. But holy women were rare, and this woman sounded to be sincere in her beliefs.

When the taxi stopped in front of a neat white house, a thin woman in her late thirties came to the door to greet Dr. Evelyn. Her light olive skin and gray-blue eyes showed that she came from the Northwest. Her brown hair was braided and tied with pink ribbons, and she could easily have passed for a European except that she wore a sari. Graciously she led Evelyn inside and seated her on a low wicker stool while she sat on a grass mat on the cement floor.

Sitting down, Evelyn shivered despite the heavy sweater she wore. It was winter, and yet here was this woman mortifying her flesh by wearing the thinnest of clothing and seating herself on the cold floor of the unheated room, hoping to gain some favor from the god she worshiped.

After the usual polite greetings had been exchanged, Dr. Evelyn asked in Hindi, "What are your symptoms?"

"I have no strength, and my blood seems to have turned to water." The woman demonstrated her lack by lifting a languid hand and letting it fall limply back into her lap. Her voice sounded tired, and she seemed to lack energy for more than the faintest smile.

Dr. Evelyn asked more questions. It soon became apparent that the woman's anemia and weakness could easily be attributed to her scanty diet.

As tactfully as her limited Hindi allowed, Dr. Evelyn told the priestess that God, the great God of heaven, loved His children and made good things for them. He did not require them to deny themselves of food or do penances to earn His favor. Carefully she explained that salvation is not obtained by our good deeds but is a free gift from God through belief in His Son, Jesus.

The woman listened and nodded, but Evelyn sensed that her polite exterior cloaked an unchanged mind. Nothing the doctor could do or say would help her. Though she should die of malnutrition, this poor soul would maintain her vow. Sadly Evelyn wrote out a prescription and closed her bag. What more could she do to bring salvation and peace to this unsatisfied soul? The hospital staff continually faced this problem— thousands of people clamoring for bodily healing but few willing to accept the soul healing found only in Christ.

Chapter 15

Twin Girls

Except for the fly buzzing irritatingly against the window screen, the afternoon siesta hour was peaceful, and Helene sat at her desk seizing the opportunity to write up patients' reports.

Suddenly she became conscious of a distant, unidentifiable sound that seemed to swell in volume and flow toward the hospital. Her window overlooked the back of the hospital compound. She could see patients' relatives sleeping curled up in whatever shade they could find on verandas or under trees. Over at the family wards a nurse quietly went about her duties. And in the dust near the well a quartet of jungle crows pecked listlessly at a piece of dry chapati. Obviously none of them heard it.

The sound swelled until it disintegrated into men's shouts and a woman's screams, and the compound leaped into life as a group of villagers burst into view dragging a protesting woman toward the hospital door. They tried to push her across the threshold, but she resisted with all her might, clutching at the doorposts with skinny fingers and trying to dig her bare, bony toes into the cement floor.

"What's the matter?" Helene's chair crashed to the floor, adding to the commotion that brought people running from all directions. Nurse Shanti had already reached the outskirts of the throng and was trying to calm them down and sort out the problem. Over her shoulder she saw Helene and relayed in English the scraps of information as she gathered them.

87

"It's a labor case—her sixth pregnancy. The others all died—born in the village. Relatives insisted she come to the hospital for this one—she's been in labor since sunrise."

Helene smiled at the relatives. This was amazing, for usually a maternity case was not brought to the hospital until the woman had wasted all her strength in days of useless labor pains and it had become obvious that something was wrong. In many cases it was too late, and not all the skill in the world could save both mother and baby. Often neither lived.

"Get her prepped, Shanti, and put her in a private room. I'll call Dr. Evelyn to come and examine her."

"A breach?" Dr. Evelyn prodded the woman's swollen body. "Or is it twins?"

She waited beside the high hospital bed, but the excitement had caused the woman's pains to cease temporarily, and it could be hours yet.

"Call me again when you need me." Evelyn hurried back to the operating theater to assist her husband with a major operation.

Sister Helene lingered, checking the woman every few minutes, but as nothing seemed to be happening, she too went back to her reports and left Shanti with the patient.

Twenty minutes later a breathless nurse rushed into the office. "Come quickly. Shanti says to hurry."

Grabbing a gown, Helene raced to the room and found the diminutive Shanti trying to hold the struggling patient down. The woman was shielding her face with her arm, screeching at the top of her voice, and trying to push herself away from the newborn baby that was lying on the bed between her legs.

Somehow they managed to hold the woman still while they tied and cut the umbilical cord and whisked the baby to safety. Helene stood back, breathless, disheveled, and indignant.

"What's the matter with her, Shanti? Why was she trying to jump off the bed? Doesn't she realize the baby would have been killed if she'd dragged it onto the cement floor?"

At first the woman would not reply. Shanti kept questioning her, probing her with words. Suddenly she poured forth a torrent of mixed abuse and explanation that made Shanti's eyes round with amazement.

"She says it's a superstition in their village that the mother must not see her new baby for twelve hours after its birth. It brings bad luck if she does. She was trying to get under the bed so she would not accidentally see the baby."

"Off that high bed!" Helene shuddered at the thought of the helpless infant dragged by the cord onto the hard floor. "What a narrow escape. Probably that's how all the others died."

She gathered the tiny baby into her arms and carried it to a cot in the nursing office, which doubled as nursery when necessary. "Too bad it's a girl, when they've had so many previous disappointments, and it's so small—I hope it will live." Leaving a junior nurse to care for the baby, Helene returned to the room in time to see the woman screw up her face in pain and begin groaning.

Fifteen minutes later another tiny girl was born, and the mother shut her eyes tightly and turned her face to the wall. Helene's lips thinned to a narrow red line as she tied the cord and handed the baby to Shanti. Wordlessly she attended to the woman and settled her into a ward bed. Then she sent a junior nurse to bring the relatives to the nursing office door.

"Two lovely, healthy little girls," she told them. Hopefully Helene searched their faces to see whether *two* live babies could atone for the fact that they were girls, but the relatives stared with hostile stolidity as if she were the one responsible for the twins not being boys.

She tried again. Singling out the father, she beckoned him to come and see his daughters, but he shrank fearfully back and tried to hide himself behind a veranda post.

The bewildered expression on Helene's face made Shanti stuff the corner of her apron into her mouth to smother her giggles, then she explained, "He won't be allowed to see them for six weeks; that's normal village custom."

There might be some sense behind that custom, Helene mused, as she lifted the mosquito netting and gazed at the squirming, red, hairy babies. Despite their ugliness she and the nurses doted on them and vied with each other for the privilege of oiling the twins and changing their cotton wrappings or feeding them warm milk from an eyedropper. Together the babies weighed a little over five pounds, and in a city hospital they would have been put into an incubator, but the mission hospital had no incubator. Loving care had to make up for the lack.

After a week, the twins' mother returned home, but Lora and Nora—as Helene dubbed them—had to remain at the hospital until Dr. Evelyn considered them strong enough to contend with the hazards of village life.

An Indian's main concern is whether the new arrival is a boy or a girl. The nurses never ceased to be amused by the European custom of asking a new baby's name. Usually Indian children of either sex are called Baba until they are three or four years old, sometimes even attending school before being addressed by a given name. To distinguish between a concentration of "Babas" they simply add their father's name and say, "Baba Presad," or "Baba Nowrangi."

90

But Helene playfully insisted that babies born in the hospital should be named. If the parents did not oblige, she would choose a name and call the infant by that name for the duration of its hospital stay. New parents somewhat familiar with Western ways sometimes decided to name their offspring after the doctors. Little brown Neales and Evelyns turned up in the most improbable places.

Eventually they sent word to the village that the twins could now go home. A whole retinue of male relatives—father, grandfathers, uncles, and cousins, with scarcely a female among them, came and triumphantly carried the babies off.

"It's like signing their death warrant to let them go," Helene mourned, wondering whether their mother would remember to sterilize the feeding bottles and prepare their formula as she had been shown. Would she boil the milk properly—and keep the flies out of it? Or would the twins get summer diarrhea and die as so many village children did?

Weeks passed. In many staff homes prayers ascended for the health and safety of the twins—prayers without much faith, it must be admitted. The chance of *two* babies surviving the change from hospital routine and strict sanitation to the haphazard habits and uncertain cleanliness of the village was exceedingly slim.

Three months later the faithless ones were ashamed when the village woman called back at the hospital to show off her twins. One of them was tied to her back, and the other naked babe was tied to its grandmother's wrinkled back. Lora and Nora, as ugly as ever, looked fat and healthy, and the nurses excitedly carried them off to be petted and admired by patients and staff alike.

Helene thought the women's visit was too good an opportunity to miss. Calling them into her office, with

Shanti interpreting, she reminded them of the five babies who had died and pointed out that these two would certainly not have survived if they had been born in the village.

To all of which the mother and the grandmother assented with vigorous headshakes and emphatic exclamations of "Jee! Jee ha."

"So you see," Helene wound up her little lecture, "what a wonderful place the hospital is. Now you go back and tell all your neighbors to come to the hospital when they are going to have babies, and tell them to bring their children here if they are sick. We want to help the village people get well, but we can't do it if they won't come to us when they're ill."

"Jee. Jee ha," they said again. Helene, feeling very pleased with herself, loaded them with tins of powdered milk and bottles of vitamins for the babies and watched them trot off toward their village.

But her confidence in her moralizing ability waned as the months passed, and no patients arrived from the twins' village.

Chapter 16

Bim, a Beggar Boy

Bim watched the car as it passed him and braked to a stop near the goldfish pond. He glimpsed white children at the windows, and instinctively he tried to quicken his progress over the grass. White children were foreigners, and foreigners meant money—white people were always rich, so his father said, and sometimes they were generous too.

Bim was a cripple. As a young boy, polio had struck him down and left his limbs twisted and useless. His father made a crude, crescent-shaped pad out of a piece of old auto tire, and sitting on that, Bim somehow managed to drag himself from place to place.

As he clumsily propelled himself along, Bim clutched a rusty can in his withered right hand. This was his beggar's tin—the sign of his profession—for every day Bim sat in the park and begged for money from the passersby. There was nothing else that a crippled twelve-year-old could do to help his father earn a living, and help he must, for Father was sick.

Father had not always been sick, just as Bim had not always been a cripple. If he tried hard, Bim could remember when the happy family lived in a village and had enough to eat and to wear and he was not a cripple. They had been poor, but by comparison with their present life it was a rich poorness. Bim remembered that years ago his father had been a vigorous, hardworking farmer, until he became ill. Because there was no doctor within many miles, he had gone for help to the village quack, who regularly prescribed all kinds of weird pills and potions made from barks and berries and frog's liver and the crushed eyes of the shy, slow-moving loris. If one could afford to pay for it, he recommended a mixture of powdered gems—diamonds, rubies, sapphires, and the like. He guaranteed this cure, but no one had been able to test his claim because no one in the village could afford such a remedy.

Father had paid for and trustingly swallowed the pills and potions, but they did no good, and daily he grew worse. The quack said someone had looked at Father with an evil eye and that no amount of medicine could combat witchcraft. So Father grew thinner and weaker, so weak that he could no longer hold the heavy wooden plow or guide the buffalo as they pulled it across the field.

Crippled Bim could not help, and the host of younger brothers and sisters were too small to be of much use. Mother slaved all the time. Bim never saw her stop. When he awoke in the morning she was already far away from the village cutting armfuls of dewy grass to feed the animals, and when darkness came and he curled up on his sleeping mat in the corner of the hut, she was still working—weaving reed baskets to sell at the weekly market.

But despite her efforts, in the end they had to leave the little farm and go to the city, where Father hoped he could find easier work.

Bim remembered the day they left. They had no furniture to move—no dishes, ornaments, books, or clothes to pack. There was nothing except Mother's few pots and pans, their sleeping mats, and Father's big used-for-everything knife. Each of them carried his mat and some other bundle on his head as they trudged the long, dusty miles to the city—each of

94

them except Bim. He had to be carried, big as he was, on his mother's hip.

In the city they found a place to live—a dirty, tumbledown hovel near the railway. But Father could not find work no matter how hard he tried, and finally, with the last money the family possessed, he walked right back to the village and bought a basketful of moorie (puffed rice) at cost. Then sitting beside a busy road he resold the rice at a small profit.

Every day he did this. Up long before dawn, he walked by starlight back to the village, bought rice from yawning villagers, walked back with the basket on his head, and sat by the roadside until the last grain was sold.

And every day the family's misery increased. They never knew what it felt like to have full stomachs; they never knew what it was like to be clothed in anything better than rags.

But still the children never tired of watching the trains go by—the long, rumbling freight trains grumbling past with their heavy loads, the happy clickety-clackety suburban trains speeding by with white-clad office workers bulging from the open doors as morning and evening they went to and from work, the huge black-engined, long-distance expresses whistling shrilly as they raced past the set signals. The children shivered with delight and forgot their hunger as they watched the trains.

But not so the weary, toilworn little woman who was their mother. The trains bustling past seemed to mock her. "An easy way out. An easy way out," their racing wheels seemed to say.

Each passing week she grew thinner and more bowed with the heaviness of her burdens until one dark night, with everyone else asleep, she slipped through the wire fence, and they reported one more "accident" on the busy tracks.

Bim, the eldest child, should by rights have assumed the household duties, with his mother gone. But what could poor crippled Bim do? The younger ones must learn to light the fire and cook the rice and wash their ragged clothes at the street pump. He would have to go out and earn money for their support.

Bim's rusty tin clanked on the cement walk as he edged his way toward the foreigners sitting in their car near the fishpond. Would they give him a lot of money? He rarely earned more than a few paisa; people always selected their smallest coins to throw to a beggar.

No one had alighted from the car, and Bim urged his weak limbs to greater effort. What if they drove away before he got there? Without a word he slid past his good friend, the gram* seller. On other days he would stop for a while and talk. With the generosity of the very poor, the gram seller would twist a scrap of newspaper into a cone and drop a handful of parched gram into it. Bim would eat it slowly and thankfully, savoring the flavor of each tiny morsel. But today he could not stop.

Ah, he was in time. Bim stopped in the shadow of the car and clanked his tin hopefully. He did not set up the whining, sniveling cry of the professional beggar because he sensed the need for a more dignified approach. He simply clanked his tin again and waited. The man and woman in the front seat talked, and Bim listened to their queer language for a while before he rattled his tin again.

The children in the back seat heard and poked their heads through the window to stare down at him. Bim stared back at them. How white they were!

---

* A legume.

96

One of the children leaned forward and tapped her mother on the shoulder.

"There's a beggar."

"I'm sorry. I don't have any money with me."

"It's a poor little crippled boy."

"I'm sorry." The woman looked down at the boy's pleading brown eyes and nudged her husband. "Have you got any money, dear?"

"Yes, I think so." The man tried to feel in his trouser pocket, but the coins had slipped so far down into the corner that he had to get out of the car before he could reach them. He brought out a handful of coins and began to drop them into the rusty tin. Suddenly he called to his wife, "Hasn't this boy got a lovely face?"

The woman turned in amazement. "I hadn't noticed." She looked critically down at Bim. "Yes, he has nice eyes and curly hair."

"But his face," the man persisted. "Don't you think he has character written on his face? I'd like to give a boy like that a chance in life."

The woman shrugged and turned back to her own children. India thronged with thousands of beggars like Bim. Why single out this one?

In awkward Hindi the man asked Bim where he lived, and Bim nodded to the row of squalid hovels across the road from the park. Then the man asked him how old he was.

"I have completed twelve years." Bim hung his head in embarrassment. He had never spoken to a white man before, and he wished the *bara-sahib* would go about his business and let him crawl home to his father with this windfall of coins.

"Do you go to school?" the man asked.

Go school? The question was so ridiculous that it took Bim some time to work out whether it was the man's halting Hindi at fault, and he really meant something else, or he understood the question correctly. He looked up at the foreigner and shook his head. Of course he didn't go to school. One needed decent clothes and books and things to go to school. Besides, he and the younger ones had to help Father. Father had never been to school either. Schooling was not for the likes of them.

"Would you like to go to school?" the man probed.

But this time Bim only stared suspiciously. Why was this foreigner asking him all these questions?

"Yes, of course he would," replied a voice behind him. It was Bim's friend, the gram seller, who had crept up and was listening intently to the conversation.

The sahib turned to him. "If I could arrange for this boy to attend a boarding school, would he go?"

"Of course he would," the gram seller nodded on Bim's behalf.

"Then I'll see what I can do." The sahib got into his car and drove away, and Bim slithered and slid his way home to tell his father the whole story and show him the tin of coins as proof that he had not been dreaming.

More than a month passed before Bim saw the sahib again. He did not know it, but letters had been flying back and forth between the missionary sahib and the principal of the nearest Seventh-day Adventist boarding school. The principal, understandably reluctant to admit an almost helpless pupil needing extra care, agreed to try it on condition that a doctor first examine the boy. "Yes," the missionary wrote back, "I have business in Banchil next month, and I shall take him to the hospital then."

Bim was out in the park begging when the car drew up in front of the row of dingy huts. The sahib and an Indian companion picked their way between the heaps of refuse, the straying dogs, the goats, and the naked children to ask for crippled Bim.

His father came out, and the Indian interpreter carefully explained that the sahib had taken a fancy to Bim and was offering to send him to school so that he would be educated and need not remain a beggar all his life. After a great deal of talking back and forth, they agreed that the missionary sahib would come the next Tuesday and take Bim.

Tuesday came, and crippled Bim was helped into the car, but oh, the poignancy of the parting. Father and son clung to each other and wept inconsolably. All the gathered neighbors and casual onlookers wept loudly—in between giving their opinions, cautions, and advice to anyone who happened to be listening. Bim's brothers and sisters wept as though he were being condemned to death.

The missionary looked perplexed and directed his interpreter to tell them that Bim didn't have to come if he didn't want to. "It's going to cost me a whole lot of money," he said, "and I'm willing to give him a chance in life if he wants it. But if he'd rather stay at home, I don't want to force him to go to school."

This message caused a great stir among the onlookers. Tears dried up like magic. The gram seller, there to see Bim off, spoke up quickly, "Yes, yes, he must go to school. His father wants him to."

So Bim set off on the greatest adventure of his young life. First the missionary took him to the bazaar and bought him new clothes, bedding, a comb, soap—things Bim had never dreamed of owning. Then they drove to the station and boarded a train, and Bim thrilled with mingled fear and joy. A train! How often he had watched the iron monsters charging past, but he never expected to ride in one himself. After an all-night journey, which seemed far too short for Bim, a taxi whisked them off toward the little mission hospital.

All the way the missionary sahib talked to Bim in halting Hindi, telling him about the God away up in the sky who loved children. He told Bim that just now they were going to visit doctors who had this God's love in their hearts and who devoted their lives to healing sick people. Perhaps God and the doctors could work a miracle and heal his crippled limbs.

Bim listened, his wide, wondering eyes fixed on the sahib's face. He did not understand all that was said, but the man's touch was gentle and his voice was kind, and Bim felt at ease.

When they reached the hospital, it seemed to Bim that everyone knew the sahib and came out to greet him. Bim found himself swept along on the same wave of enthusiastic friendliness. In no time at all he was bathed, fed, and being examined in the doctor's office.

"See," said Dr. Neale as he tapped the boy's knee with a little hammer, "the reflexes are not entirely gone. There is some life in the worst leg, only a little, but . . . Where's Evelyn?"

Dr. Evelyn came in, and the two doctors talked for a long time, tapping and questioning and looking so serious that Bim almost became frightened. At length they turned to the sahib and said, "It will take a long time and cost a lot of money, but we think he can be taught to use his limbs again, with massage, physiotherapy, iron braces, good food. Anyway, don't send him to the boarding school—leave him here. He can use the hospital wheelchair and attend our Hindi day school while we treat him. With God's help, who knows what might happen?"

Six weeks passed, and for Bim the novelty began to wear off. No miracle happened—the doctors did not produce some magic cure whereby Bim's crippled limbs suddenly became straight and strong. Instead, there were those painful periods called "treatments"

100

when nurses patiently worked over him for hours, pommeling, pounding, pulling.

And school held no magic either. The other children could hold pencils and color pictures and write words, but Bim could not. They could read stories from brightly colored books that they called primers—Bim could not. He stared long and hard at the queer little marks on the pages of the ABC book the teacher gave him, but not a word did they say to him. Why did books speak to the other children and not to him?

Bim began to think longingly of home. He did not remember the dirt and squalor of the hovel near the railway tracks. He remembered only the noisy welcome his younger brothers and sisters gave him when he crawled home at night with his begging tin of coins.

He forgot that back in the city his stomach almost always ached with hunger. He thought only of the good times—the pujas once a year when Father somehow found enough money to buy a little goat's meat for a curry, and a little sugar to sprinkle on chapati. How good it tasted! So much nicer than the good, strengthening food the doctors gave him: milk, eggs, vegetables, to "build him up" they said. Bim did not want to be built up; he wanted to go home.

Nobody knows by what process of mental telepathy, or other means, Bim's discontent was conveyed to his father. But one day Father, sick and ragged and thin, appeared at the hospital door to take Bim home.

Bim welcomed him jubilantly and excitedly directed the cramming of all his new possessions into a hospital pillow slip. With the improvised cloth sack balanced on his head and Bim on his back, Father trudged off down the dusty road, and there wasn't a thing the hospital could do about it.

When the missionary sahib heard what had happened, he called at the little hovel by the railway tracks. But he was received coldly, and the omnipresent gram seller explained with a shrug: "He wanted to come home; they missed each other. What to do?"

Chapter 17

Little Prakash Peter

The housephone jangled harshly and shattered the dark stillness of the bedroom. Without opening her eyes, Helene lifted her head and listened.

Br-r-r-ring, br-r-r-ring, br-ring. "Two longs and a short—it's mine." She slid weary feet into her slippers and stumbled into the hallway, switching on the light with one hand and reaching for the telephone with the other.

"Yes?"

"Oh, matron, a new patient has been brought in, a delivery case. I've put her in the linen room until you come."

"How far is she?"

"I haven't examined her. I thought you . . ."

"All right. I'll come."

Helene yawned and looked at her watch. Eleven o'clock. It was less than two hours since she had left the hospital and come home to prepare and eat her solitary supper. "And I began work at 6:30 this morning," she yawned again. "No forty-hour week in the mission field."

She dressed quickly, and the screen door banged behind her as she stepped off the veranda and shone her flashlight onto the crooked track that led to the hospital. Snakes were not common on this densely populated compound, but they were not uncommon either, and she shuddered as she remembered the green snake that had been discovered sliding noiselessly through the window of the nursing office.

103

When the girls inside screamed, one of the orderlies dashed outside and slammed the window shut on it.

"It must have come out of these lovely bougainvillea vines that twine over the hospital porch." She beamed her flashlight onto the purple flowers and jumped in fright as the lonely night nurse greeted her from the shadows.

"Oh, matron, I'm glad you've come. She's making an awful fuss, and I can't get my work done."

Helene made a wry face. "These village people are a queer mixture, Pris. Some of them will bear terrible agony with the fortitude of a bronze statue, and others fuss and cry over a cut finger."

"This woman's only skin and bone, poor thing. Her relatives say that she has been sick for a long time."

"I wish they would bring pregnant women in for prenatal care"—Helene sighed as she followed Pris along the veranda—"instead of blaming the hospital if the mother or baby dies even after we have done everything possible."

She drew aside the curtain of the linen storeroom, which was often used in an emergency until a ward bed became vacant, and said over her shoulder, "Please set up a tray and bring it in."

Looking down at the suffering woman, Helene guessed that she was in her thirties, but her face was prematurely aged by hard work and drawn by lines of pain. She was so thin that Helene wondered how such a pitiful creature could have carried a pregnancy so far.

When Pris returned with a dressing tray, Helene eased a rubber glove onto her right hand and made an examination. "I think she'll be some time yet. The poor woman is too weak to make much effort. Keep an eye on her, and call me again when you think it's necessary. I'll give her a sedative before I go, Pris. Do

104

you have time to heat some milk for her?"

"Yes, matron. Everyone's settled down except No. 11. He had surgery this morning, and he's having a lot of pain."

"I'll look in on him before I leave." Helene stifled another yawn. "Good night, nurse."

"Good night, matron."

Only one trained nurse and a junior aide could be spared for the night shift, and the night watchman who patrolled the hospital grounds every hour was supposed to assist them wherever possible. Unfortunately, having a bad habit of sneaking off to some secluded corner and taking a nap whenever he felt like it, he could never be found when needed.

So it came about that when Nurse Pris checked the new patient at 4 AM and decided that the matron's presence was needed, the night watchman could not be located. Instead of being awakened by his gentle tapping on her front door, Helene was again jarred into consciousness by the telephone's harsh summons.

"Yes?"

"I think you'd better come over. She seems to be making progress now."

The pale light of dawn guided Helene's footsteps along the crooked path, and the distant sounds of roosters and cattle and the smell of smoky cooking fires told her that she was not the only one whose working day had begun.

Two hours later the day staff came on duty and found the nursing office empty. Through the windows the huge overhead light in the operating theater, which also served as labor ward, gleamed brighter than the early morning sun.

"Must be an emergency," they decided, nodding to one another. "Let's see if Pris got her charting done beforehand."

But before they could investigate the charts, Pris rushed into the office, cap awry and uniform stained. "Take care of this baby," she panted as she thrust a mewling, towel-wrapped bundle into the arms of the nearest nurse. "I've got to go back. Matron needs help."

She rushed off, and the nurses crowded around as Nelia tenderly laid the mite in a crib that was always kept on hand in the office. "It's a boy," she told them as she reached for the olive oil and cotton. "He doesn't look too good to me; he's terribly thin and lethargic. Poor little pet!"

The others crooned over the baby in typical feminine fashion until Dr. Evelyn's warning footsteps sent them scurrying off to their work.

At midmorning a group of villagers appeared to ask about the new patient and her baby. Dr. Evelyn had bad news for them. "The poor woman has tuberculosis in a very bad form and needs special treatment, which we cannot give her here. There is a sanatorium in town, and I will make arrangements to have her transferred there."

The villagers shrugged and spread their hands wide in the customary gesture of resignation, and Dr. Evelyn went on. "She had a normal delivery; so the day after tomorrow you may call a taxi and take her to Dr. Sen at the sanatorium. He is a fine doctor and will do his best to save her."

"What about the baby?" One of the women in the group clutched Evelyn's white coat with a grubby hand. "May we take him home?"

Dr. Evelyn shook her head. "We will keep him here and do our best, but right now he needs a blood transfusion to give him a start. Which of you is his father?"

In a commotion the villagers pushed a jungly looking man forward. Evelyn spoke slowly in Hindi

106

and then had one of the nurses repeat her words in local dialect to make sure that the man understood what she was saying. "Your baby is very weak, and he needs a blood transfusion. Let us test your blood to see if it will match his."

The man drew back and stuttered fearfully, "Not now. I will come in two hours."

"But it will only take a minute, and it does not hurt you. Only the tiniest prick, and it might save your baby's life, your son's life," Evelyn emphasized, knowing the high value placed on sons in this part of India.

But the terrified man edged his way through the crowd of onlookers still muttering that he would return in two hours.

Dr. Evelyn sighed in defeat. She knew very well that she would not see him again. But to save face, when the two hours had elapsed, she asked the lingering villagers where the father was.

"He had to return to the village," they chorused. "But he will give blood for his son another day. Today is not propitious. Next week . . ."

"The baby may not live until next week."

The villagers shrugged and remained unmoved when Evelyn pleaded that one of them volunteer to give blood for the baby. "It is the father's duty," they said and turned their backs. They were there to prepare meals for the patient, and that was all.

Speechless with frustration, Dr. Evelyn turned away. Knowing it was useless to argue, she felt crushed and helpless. At the door she met Helene. "I heard them. Let me give it—I'm the same blood group as the baby."

The transfusion worked wonders, and the fragile infant began his fight for life. Twice in the weeks that followed, it looked as if the battle would be lost, but again the precious life-giving blood seeped gener-

107

ously from Helene's arm into his pale thin body, and he fought anew.

At first an eyedropper of milk filled his tiny stomach. As his need for nourishment increased, the baby learned to suck a feeding bottle, and the nurses vied with one another for the privilege of feeding him his formula.

Nothing more was heard from villagers or relatives after they took the mother away, and when Dr. Evelyn finally phoned the sanatorium for news, she was told that they had insisted on taking the woman home after only a few weeks of treatment. "They said that women were easier to come by than money to pay for her treatment," informed the voice at the other end of the line. "It is almost certain that she would be dead by now because she was in an advanced stage of tuberculosis."

So there was nothing the hospital could do but keep the baby alive. As soon as he was old enough to recognize faces he showed a distinct preference for Helene, the white face among the brown ones who ministered to his needs. Helene spoiled him outrageously. When she went on rounds with doctor, she carried the little fellow with her, and if he seemed at all restless or fretful, she took him home with her when she went off duty. She was alone in a foreign land, far from relatives and friends, and the baby helped her fill the aching loneliness she often felt.

"There's a lot of my blood in that baby's veins," she pointed out when the nurses giggled and teased her, "and I'm going to name him. I think I'll call him Prakash; that's a fine Indian name." But very few of the staff called him Prakash; he was usually known as "Matron Helene's baby."

When little Prakash became strong enough to go home, the hospital secretary wrote to the village and told the father to come and take the baby, but there was no reply. He waited a month and then sent another letter. And another. He sent verbal messages by the occasional patient who came from the same village, but still there was no reply.

The months flew by. Little Prakash learned to smile and coo, to sit and stand and gurgle and creep and do all the adorable tricks that babies the world over do, but still no one claimed him.

The hospital secretary, the business manager, the doctors, and Helene conferred about the problem and agreed to send one more letter by registered mail. "I'll tell the relatives that the baby will be given out for adoption if he is not claimed within one month." The business manager avoided Helene's pleading eyes. "We can't keep him here forever; his account is almost into four figures now."

Again there was no reply, but a few weeks after the letter was sent, a group of men appeared at the hospital and said that they were relatives who had come to take the baby. The child's father was not among them, and the group appeared uncertain as to his whereabouts. They did not know whether the baby's mother was alive or dead. In fact their answers to every question were so vague and unsatisfactory that they aroused suspicion.

The staff knew that certain criminal gangs specialized in kidnapping small children and selling them as slaves, or to wealthy childless couples, and they felt sure that these shifty-eyed individuals were up to no good. But they could not prove it, nor could they think up any reason why little Prakash should not be handed over to them. For over an hour they discussed the matter and wondered what to do. Then the business manager had a brilliant idea: the account!

He sprang to the cabinet and leafed through the file marked "Unpaid Accounts" until he came to the one for Prakash, and while the others watched anxiously he stepped onto the veranda and handed the bill to the waiting group. "You may take the child as soon as you have paid this account," he said with a disarming smile.

The men looked at one another. They looked at the account, and then mumbling some excuses about not having so much money with them and promising to bring it later on, without further ado the group of "relatives" disappeared.

Three months sped by, and still the problem of what to do with little Prakash remained unsolved. There was no lack of wealthy Muslims or Hindus who wanted to adopt him, but Helene refused to let him go to anyone but a Seventh-day Adventist.

Word was carried far and wide; letters were sent and answers received. Many, many families would have welcomed the little boy, but poverty was the bar.

"We need a Seventh-day Adventist orphanage here," Helene thought as she leaned over the crib and spooned mashed banana into Prakash's eager mouth. "If only I had the faith to start one myself, like Müller or Dr. Barnado." She sighed and kissed the little boy on the top of his head. "I wish I could adopt you myself, Prakash, but the government would never let you leave the country when it came time for me to return to my homeland."

The little fellow looked up with wondering eyes as he felt a warm tear splash onto his head. Helene was the only mother he knew, and he could not bear to see her unhappy. Unsteadily he clung to the crib rail and pulled himself to his feet. "Da-da, ba-ba-ba," he gabbled in universal baby language and held out his chubby arms to her.

Two weeks after Prakash's first birthday the unexpected happened. A letter arrived from a pastor in a distant city. "None of the Indian families in this church can take the baby you mentioned, but there is a part European family who only have one child. They are fine people, but I don't know whether they would be willing to adopt a full-blooded Indian baby. Shall I ask them? At worst they can only say no."

But they did not say no, and never was a baby boy more welcome. Within a week all arrangements had been made, and they came to the hospital to spend some time with the baby so that he could get accustomed to his new parents before being taken to live in the city and becoming Peter, the much-loved son of a highly esteemed church elder.

Chapter 18

Hospital Hideout

As soon as she saw the new patient, Helene had a "feeling" about him. There was something unusual, something amiss, but what? She could not tell.

"Just a woman's intuition," she scolded herself, trying to shrug off the feeling as she picked up his chart.

"Hmm, fever. They all have that. It's so common over here that it's hardly an ailment at all. 'Temperature 99.9.' That's not very high. He could easily have run that up by drinking hot tea at the café across the road before he came in here. 'Cold chills.' That can't be proved. I have a feeling that this fellow is deceiving us for some reason. He begged to be admitted to the hospital, and Dr. Neale is so tenderhearted that he couldn't refuse. I think I'll keep an eye on this patient; he's up to something."

Every morning when Helene accompanied Dr. Neale on his rounds, the patient had some trifling new symptom to report, but although Dr. Neale examined him carefully and ordered numerous tests, he could find nothing organically wrong and after a few days ordered his discharge.

The displeased patient, not wanting to leave the hospital, argued and pleaded and vowed that his aches and pains were eased only while he lay in bed. He was deaf to the doctor's explanation that his bed was needed for a seriously ill patient, and when the next pulse and temperature charting revealed that his temperature had risen slightly, Dr. Neale relented and reluctantly allowed him to stay another day or two.

All this increased Helene's feeling that something was wrong. She noticed that this patient did not have visitors come to see him. He had no relatives staying with him to make his bed, do his washing, and cook his food (not that he needed anyone to do anything for him, because there was nothing at all wrong with him; she was convinced of that). All his meals were brought to him from the little tea shop across the road. He was well dressed, he had plenty of money to pay his hospital account, he troubled no one, and outwardly he appeared no different from any of the other men in the ward. But Helene was convinced that he *was* different.

After two days Dr. Neale again tried to discharge the young man. Again his temperature rose slightly, and he begged to stay on in the hospital, and again the softhearted doctor agreed. This was repeated once more. The "mystery" man's stay had lengthened into three weeks when, as Helene walked through the male ward, she was surprised to see another youth sitting by the bed. She noted that they both looked extremely worried and wondered why, but in the bustle of hospital activity she forgot the incident until the next afternoon when she walked into the male ward and was shocked to see the "mystery" man sitting up in bed wearing handcuffs.

Two policemen stood by the bed firing questions at him, and the visitor of the day before was standing at the ward door talking to Dr. Abil.

Since Dr. Neale and Dr. Evelyn were away on a trip, an Indian couple, Doctors Abil and Shela Chand, were in charge of the hospital.

For a few minutes Helene stood watching the visitor gesticulating wildly and rattling on in his mother tongue. She could not understand what he was saying, but she gathered by the tone of his voice and his actions that he was trying to persuade the doctor to do something, and he was refusing. Speculating about this unexpected turn of events, she walked out to the veranda and almost bumped into Dr. Shela.

"Something's going on in there." Helene nodded her head and indicated the ward she had just left. "You'd better go in and see if your husband needs any help. Those men are up to no good."

Dr. Shela peered around the door. The sight of policemen and handcuffs in a hospital ward startled her. At the other end of the ward the "mystery" man's visitor was still clutching the doctor's arm and talking in an urgent tone. With fear in her eyes, Dr. Shela hurried to her husband's side.

Half an hour later she came to the nursing office to tell Helene what she had found out. "You were right—they're a bad lot. That fellow was trying to persuade Abil to certify that the patient is insane."

"Why?"

"I didn't get all the details, but it seems that he is a good friend of our mysterious patient, and the patient is wanted for murder."

"What?" Helene nearly dropped the armful of charts she was holding.

"Yes. He killed and robbed an old lady in Allahabad and then absconded up here. He had planned it well. He'd heard about our hospital, and he decided that if he pretended to be sick and stayed in the hospital for a month or so, no one would think of looking for him here, and by then he'd be fairly safe."

"Very clever, using our hospital as a hideout and preying on Doctor's good nature. Right from the start I felt there was something strange about that fellow. It just goes to show . . ."

Exactly what it went to show Dr. Shela did not find out, because at that juncture she was called to attend a sick child; but next day she poked her head around

114

the nursing-office door to tell Helene the end of the story.

"The policemen took that patient off to prison, but his friend came here again this morning trying to persuade Abil to certify that the patient is insane. I suppose he'd get a much lighter sentence that way."

"I suppose so." Helene tapped her pen on the edge of the desk and added dryly, "I wonder what Dr. Neale will say when he returns and hears all about this."

"Can't fool a woman's sixth sense, can you?" chuckled Dr. Shela, and brown eyes met blue with an understanding twinkle.

Chapter 19

The Little Burned Girl

With a skill born of long practice, Amira patted and shaped the mass of cow dung heaped on the ground in front of her, sprinkling water from a rusty old can and kneading until she had the right consistency to make it into smooth round balls, which she rolled between the palms of her hands.

With the last ball rolled and set out, she sat back on her heels and surveyed her handiwork with a satisfied air. But the job was not finished yet. Picking up a ball in each hand she slapped them onto the mud-brick wall of the house, pressing each one firmly and leaving a distinctive five-finger pattern in the soft manure. Soon row upon row of moist rounds decorated the wall. They would dry out in the sun and adhere to the wall until needed for fuel. Animal manure provided the main source of cooking fuel for poor people like Amira's family, and the women and girls of the household kept a constant supply stuck to walls or nearby tree trunks.

When the last round was in place, Amira cleaned her hands on a patch of grass and wiped them on the end of her long sari. Actually she was too young to be wearing a sari. Girls usually wear short dresses until they reach marriageable age, but the very poor are glad for any sort of covering, and Amira's ragged sari was the only clothing she possessed.

The lengthening shadows of palm trees warned the little girl that it would soon be too dark to work, and her weary parents would be coming from the fields, expecting to find their supper ready.

During rice planting, every able-bodied adult worked from sunrise to sunset preparing the ground and carefully terracing it so that precious water could pass from plot to plot. Rice means food, clothing, and livelihood to the villagers, and everything else is secondary. Boys helped their parents in the fields, and girls minded the babies and prepared the food.

Hurrying now, Amira reached for a woven leaf tray and measured onto it three handfuls of rice for each family member. In the doorway she squatted on her haunches and rhythmically tossed the tray until the particles of dirt and grit separated from the grain and could be swept away. As she worked she called shrilly to little sister to fetch water from the village well.

"Juldi, Juldi. Hurry," she urged. "The rice is done, and I am waiting."

An overturned pan protected the mound of white grains from marauding chickens while Amira crumbled dried dung cakes into the bucket-shaped clay cookstove, topped them with a layer of charcoal and a sprinkle of kerosene, and struck a match.

While the rice boiled she peeled onions with skillful fingers, and when little sister came with the heavy water jar on her head, Amira helped lift it to the ground. The two children giggled and dawdled over their work as children do the world over. Amira pulled little sister's hair, little sister tagged Amira, and a merry chase began inside the tiny hut.

As Amira dodged around the clay stove her trailing sari swept unnoticed across a tongue of flame licking up the side of the rice pot. Instantly flames leaped up the flimsy cloth, and the terrified girls ran screaming from the hut.

Their shrieks spurred the returning villagers, and within minutes brave hands threw Amira to the ground and rolled her agonized body in the dust. Later little sister sobbed out her story to their frantic parents.

Owls were hooting dismally in the pipal trees when Helene finally left the hospital, kicked off her shoes, and slumped onto her bed, too tired to prepare and eat her lonely supper. Her day's work had been hectic, and all she wanted was rest and peace, but her taut nerves had scarcely begun to relax when the telephone's shrill peal split the silence of her bungalow.

Mechanically she counted the rings—two long and one short.

"Mine," she sighed wearily and swung her legs over the side of the bed.

"Matron, there's a villager here telling me something about someone being burned, but I can't make head or tail of it. He doesn't speak *pukka* Hindi. It must be some sort of local dialect."

"Well, I don't speak any local dialect either," replied Helene pointedly.

"Yes, I know. But . . ." The voice at the other end trailed off uncertainly, and in imagination Helene could see the night nurse wringing her hands.

"All right. I'll come over."

Easing her aching feet back into their shoes, she picked up a flashlight and stumbled down the steps.

By the time she arrived at the nursing station the villager had been joined by another man, and several relatives of inpatients were all talking at once, trying to help sort out the message. The nurse turned thankfully to her superior and remarked, "He says it's a young girl who has been burned."

"From hip to heel," put in a patient's relative.

"Her sari caught on fire," explained another, and then the whole group began to talk and explain and jabber among themselves until Helene raised her voice above the hubbub and asked, "Where is she? In what village did all this happen?"

The babel broke out afresh, and finally the information was gathered and imparted: "In Kuthi village."

"How far away is that?"

"Oh, it's quite near." Half a dozen hands pointed out the direction.

"Then will they bring her to the hospital, or do they want someone to go the village and treat her burns there?"

The question was interpreted to the messengers with the usual variations and explanations and jabbering back and forth. Then from several eager tongues came the astonishing answer, "No need to go. She is here, waiting at the hospital gate."

For a moment Helene was speechless, then both tongue and feet galvanized into action. "Bring her inside. How thoughtless you are," she cried as her racing feet carried her to the front gate where a rickshaw was waiting. Two shrouded figures sat in the rickshaw awkwardly supporting the fainting, whimpering little girl.

"She is so badly burned that she cannot sit down," one of them explained to the night nurse and the rest of the curious onlookers who had followed.

"And you kept her waiting in agony all this time. Why didn't you bring her straight in or say at once that she was here?" Helene reprimanded the villagers, but the men gaped at her vacantly—they knew no English.

"Call Dr. Evelyn. Bring a cart. Where's the night watchman?" Issuing orders right and left, Helene dashed back into the hospital to prepare a pain-killing injection before treating the injured child.

Hours later when the dreadful burns had been

dressed and Amira, mercifully sedated, lay comfortably in the first bed she had ever known, Dr. Evelyn wrote her report: "Shock, third degree burns over a large area of hips and legs." And to Helene she said, "We've done our best, but I doubt that she will pull through." Tapping her cheek with the end of the pen, she thought for a while and then added, "She might, though. She's a game little lass."

As the pain-filled weeks passed, Amira became the hospital pet. Doctors and the matron rarely passed her bed without some little treat for her. The children from the nearby mission station felt sorry that she had to stay in bed hour after hour, day after day, with nothing to do. Her mother always sat by her side saying nothing, doing nothing, except to care for Amira's physical needs. There were no pretty bed jackets, no toys, no books, no games, and no puzzles to help the little girl while away the long hours. The children wished they could give her books, but she could not read. They wished they could talk to her, but she could not understand.

So they made used Christmas cards into scrapbooks, and Amira amused herself looking at the pictures (often held upside down) of incomprehensible things like snow and sleds and Christmas trees and Santa Claus.

Amira's little sister spent a lot of time at the hospital, too, standing quietly by Amira's bed and watching the nurses come and go. When Sabbath came, the nurses took her to the primary division and urged her to join the staff children in their brightly decorated room. At first she hung back, scarcely daring to peep around the door at the wonders within, but gradually curiosity overcame her, and step by cautious step she ventured inside and sat on the straw mat at the very edge of the wriggling throng.

The finger plays and songs, the Bible stories and

the activities, fascinated little sister. Never in all her life had she held a colored pencil in her hand, and her awkward scribblings back and forth across the paper were anything but artistic. But she proudly showed her effort to Mother and Amira and excitedly told them all she had seen and done.

Her eager reports made Amira long to attend, and as soon as she could bear to be moved, kind hands carried her along to see the pictures and flannel-graphs and hear the stories of Jesus' love. Mother went to church too. She sat with the nurses on the women's side, listening and looking. She was a Hindu because she had been born into a Hindu family, but her religion meant only that she must place daily offerings—a few grains of rice or beans, a single flower plucked from a jungle tree—in front of the little image that stood in a niche of the mud-brick wall of her hut. In some vague way she knew that she did it to keep evil away from the family—the evil eye, spells, black magic. She had never heard of the God who loved people, who did them good and not evil. Silently Amira's mother listened and learned.

After six months in the hospital, Amira returned home, badly scarred but walking as well as ever. It was little wonder that the previously hostile villagers welcomed the hospital staff when they arranged to hold a branch Sabbath School in Kuthi. Every Sabbath afternoon Amira and her mother and little sister and all the uncles and aunts and cousins sat right up at the front of the crowd that gathered to listen.

Chapter 20

Cardiac Arrest

The three wealthy Lal brothers lived in the Banchil district. Their wives had borne children, but there was only one boy among the many girls, little Babu Lal.

In typical fashion the three families—including parents, parents-in-law, uncles, aunts, cousins, and other distant and nondescript relatives—lived in one huge mansion. They had all things common. Everyone went in and out of everyone else's apartments and knew everyone else's business. Family privacy was unknown.

Small wonder that in such a situation the one little boy became the spoiled darling of the whole clan. In whichever apartment he chose to reside the entire household became his willing slaves. He was chief heir to the property of all three Lal brothers, and he in turn was the property of all.

The wife of one of the brothers was particularly devoted to the little boy and spoiled him outrageously. But she got tuberculosis and had to spend months in a private suite at the mission hospital. This meant a long separation from her beloved nephew, and as soon as she was allowed home again she insisted that he come and live with her to make up for the lost time.

Babu Lal had a dropped eyelid that did not interfere with his sight, but it did slightly mar his looks. His doting auntie decided that the problem should be rectified. During her stay in the mission hospital she had heard about the coming of a foreign eye team. She decided that this opportunity must not be missed.

What went on at home when she announced this decision, we do not know. But one day Auntie decked herself out in rustling silken sari and jewels worth a prime minister's ransom. Then with satin-clad nephew at her side she rode away in dignified state in a chauffeur-driven jalopy that would have been scrap material in a more fortunate country. They arrived at the hospital entrance in a flurry of dust and self-importance.

The eye specialist examined the boy and explained that a simple operation could tighten the muscle of the drooping eyelid. Auntie beamed. The specialist told her to fill in the form and have the boy admitted to the hospital for a few days. Auntie beamed again and reached for the printed paper.

But a hitch arose when she came to the last item on the form—the space reserved for the father's signature consenting to the operation. The child's father was on a business trip and knew nothing of his sister-in-law's plan. She waved a bejeweled hand negatively. No, they could not possibly write and explain it all to him, procuring his consent in the short time available. Besides it wasn't at all necessary. Her own husband, the brother of the child's father, would give his consent.

The eye specialist explained that the hospital must have the consent of the child's *own* father before he could touch the child. "Suppose something went wrong. The parents would blame me or the hospital. They might take legal proceedings."

Auntie snorted and wiped her nose with the end of her silken sari. A father's brother's signature was just as good—more than adequate. What could go wrong in a simple operation like fixing up an eyelid? Pshaw! The child's sight was not endangered. She herself would take full responsibility. Had she not been a patient in this hospital for many months? She knew what good care would be taken of the child. She would . . .

And so it went on for more than half an hour. Both sides gave their point of view over and over, the doctor patiently; the aunt dramatically. At last the visiting specialist's resistance wore down. Against his better judgment he accepted Auntie's promise of her husband's signature of consent. After all, it was only a minor operation.

On the day of the little boy's operation Helene and Dr. Hexham, who was acting as hospital superintendent while Doctors Neale and Evelyn were away on leave, assisted the visiting eye specialist. Three cataracts had been successfully removed and a squint corrected, and then Babu Lal was brought in.

His was only a very minor operation, and with practiced hands the specialist quickly tightened the lax muscle. The incision was being closed when, without warning, the child's heart stopped beating.

Instantly the operation halted. Every person in the theater caught his breath. They watched in agonized suspense as Dr. Hexham made an incision in the child's chest and began to massage his heart. The doctor's gloved fingers moved rhythmically. He had eight minutes in which to save the boy's life. Only eight minutes. Longer than that would be too late.

Three minutes passed. Four. The heart remained inert. The air in the theater was electric with suspense as the nurses and the specialist watched the race with death.

Five minutes. Silent, frantic prayers for help ascended from the mission staff. Who knew at what precise instant the boy's heart had stopped beating? Maybe there were not even three minutes left. Perhaps only two, or less—maybe one.

124

Beads of perspiration shone on Dr. Hexham's brow above his mask as he massaged and prayed, massaged and prayed. Then gratitude flooded through him as he felt the vital muscle throb weakly under his searching fingers. Erratically at first but then with steady, strengthening rhythm, the boy's heart resumed its task, and the theater staff relaxed. With the operation concluded, Babu Lal was wheeled into his private room.

With his condition still precarious, the nursing supervision took it in turns to stay beside his bed day and night. Auntie, flattered by all the attention given to her precious nephew, did not dream that he had come so close to death.

She eased her silken bulk into a wicker chair and waved her plump hands heavenward as she volubly called upon her gods to witness the cleverness of these foreigners and their devotion to duty. She didn't know that they had prayed, were still praying, to the true God who alone held the child's life in His hands.

And their prayers were answered. Little Babu Lal continued to improve, and the next day he was pronounced "out of danger."

But the episode caused great distress among the hospital personnel. The visiting specialist blamed himself, insisting, "It was all my fault. I should never have listened to that woman and let her persuade me. Suppose the boy had died. What good would an uncle's signature have been?"

Everyone nodded solemnly, and Helene shuddered at the thought of what might have been: the relatives' grief, the accusations, the despair, the endless court cases. How gracious their heavenly Father was!

She closed her eyes and offered a silent prayer of gratitude. When she opened them, the specialist was looking at her. "Yes," he nodded humbly, "I know it

125

was the prayers that did it. I'm not a professing Christian, but I feel as if I'm walking on holy ground around this hospital."

Chapter 21

No Forty-Hour Week

Hospital personnel changes: doctors and nurses, chaplain and staff, patients and their relatives, come and go, but the spirit of the hospital staff remains the same.

This spirit prompts tired nurses and other staff members to go from ward to ward each Friday evening, bringing to the patients the gospel story in song.

The spirit motivates those same tired persons, or others just as weary, to walk miles in the scorching summer sun or biting winter wind to conduct Sabbath afternoon meetings in friendly villages.

The same spirit inspires hardworking staff members to go the second mile. No one is ever too tired or too busy to call back on a patient when working hours are over. Perhaps a Bible study at night will fan into flaming desire for salvation that tiny spark of interest shown during a morning conversation at treatment time.

The spirit moves staff members to assist the chaplain in his twice-weekly meetings in the wards—setting up projector and filmstrips, translating, explaining, helping.

This same spirit impels the European doctors in their rare hours off duty to hold clinics in nearby villages while the national assistants preach to the assembled villagers in their own tongue.

Take away this spirit and what remains is worthless. Healing of body without attempting to heal the soul is work only half done.

No, there is no forty-hour week for dedicated workers. Only the great record books of heaven will adequately tell the story of the good that has been accomplished by this little mission hospital and the hundreds of similar hospitals and clinics of all faiths the world over.